The Women You Were Warned About

Answers to Absent Questions

C. S. Barnes

The Women You Were Warned About

Answers to Absent Questions

First published in April 2017 by Black Pear Press
www.blackpear.net

Copyright © C.S. Barnes 2017

All rights reserved.

No part of this publication may be reproduced, copied, stored in a retrieval system, or transmitted in any form or by any means without prior permission in writing from the copyright holder. Nor may it be otherwise circulated in any form or binding or cover other than the one in which it is published and without conditions including this condition being imposed on subsequent purchasers.

All the characters in this publication, other than those clearly in the public domain, are fictitious and any resemblance to real persons, living or dead, is purely coincidental.

ISBN 978-1-910322-49-9

Cover design by C.S. Barnes and Daniel Tryner.

Black Pear Press

Introduction

The Women You Were Warned About was initially a short and experimental prose project written under the title, *Brief Interviews with Hideous Women*. After reading David Foster Wallace's critically acclaimed collection *Brief Interviews with Hideous Men* during my studies for my Masters degree, I became enamoured not only with his form—of allowing characters to provide answers for absent questions—but also by his increasingly disturbing portrayals of male characters. I remember thinking then, 'Why is it always the men? Why is it never the hideous women?'

As my academic endeavours continued both my research and my creative writing were constantly coming back to these same two questions. I found myself increasingly frustrated by the absence of unpleasant female characters in fiction and so, when the opportunity arose to expand my interviews into something longer, I grabbed greedily at it with both hands. The interviews were integrated into the larger text in a way that allows them to act as pit stops between the longer stretches of narrative. The questions in every sequence are deliberately absent; while it is possible to determine what has been asked, it was constructed as such to allow the women and their stories to be the dominant voices.

These interviews acted as a foundation on which to stack the rest of the collection from then on. In some instances I attempted to adhere to the traditional short story format, which you will find in the likes of (Not) Guilty and Mercy, Mercy, while other stories are told through more experimental means. Fancy Seeing You Here was, after much redrafting, eventually written as a short script, while Hallelujah encourages you to pick your own ending (there is a happy option in there, I promise). The manipulation of form is for two reasons; primarily, I am all too aware that these are unconventional stories and for that reason, I felt they deserved some unconventional telling. Secondly, I hoped, and still hope, to remind readers that the short story format holds endless possibilities and, contrary to popular belief, it can be so much more than a convenient alternative to reading a novel.

This collection has been two years in the making and, during that time, I have become surprisingly attached to my motley crew of unsavoury women. If nothing else I hope that one day this collection, and the women housed within it, can cause similar stirs of emotion for those reading as the ones I experienced when writing. These women may be hideous but it is my firm belief that many of them are also real; you may even know some of them…

Acknowledgements

This book was born in the Creative Writing department at the University of Birmingham. It started in a seminar and it finished in a dissertation session, and I will be forever grateful to this department for giving my horrible women a space to stamp their feet.

Additional thanks, of course, must go to Black Pear Press for publishing this. These women have been written, re-shaped, and made much more hideous than they were in the first draft, and I must thank Polly Stretton, Tony Judge, and Rod Griffiths for their guidance and support in getting this collection to print.

Thank you to my partner-in-crime, not only for designing the cover of this book but for listening to rants and for easing worries. We talk about feminism and horrible women far more than we should have to, and I am absurdly grateful for that. Thank you, mush. Always.

And finally, to the least horrible women I know—my wonderful mum and my beautiful sister—thank you for supporting me in this and everything else I have ever written. I am pleased to say that you are not in these pages, but these pages would certainly not exist without you.

Contents

Introduction iii
Acknowledgements v
Contents vi
An On-Going Interview with the Narrator 1
Brief Interviews With Hideous Women 6
    Interview One 6
    Interview Two 8
    Interview Three 10
    Interview Four 13
An On-Going Interview with the Narrator 15
(Not) Guilty 18
Oh, Oh, What A Difference A Day Makes 25
Mercy, Mercy 31
Brief Interviews With Hideous Women (2) 50
    Interview Five 50
    Interview Six 51
    Interview Seven 53
A Little Too Relaxed 56
Fancy Seeing You Here 63
An On-Going Interview with the Narrator 68
Hallelujah 71
Starting Young 80
Brief Interviews with Hideous Women (3) 89
    Interview Eight 89
    Interview Nine 92
    Interview Ten 95
    Interview Eleven 97
An On-Going Interview with the Narrator 99
A Portrait Of Old Age (1) 103
A Portrait Of Old Age (2) 108
A Portrait Of Old Age (3) 112
A Portrait Of Old Age (4) 117
You Are Saying… 123
An On-Going Interview with the Narrator—A Conclusion 128

An On-Going Interview with the Narrator

Q.
'And I suppose that's where I come in, is it? No one likes a grass, you know. If I wasn't so tired of this place then I wouldn't be doing this at all. You're just giving me something to do. I don't even know what you think you're getting at with this book.'

Q.

'Pff, no one'll believe that.'

Q.

'Because no one believes anything bad of women. That's why this place is so fuckin' popular; no one can quite believe what goes on behind the walls, you know. Meek and mild women who can't do this, that, or the other, and that's what people will think. Fiction or not, people will see a catchy title about terrible women, or hideous women, whatever it was, they'll pick it up, glance at the back, maybe, and think— Well, that sounds a little too farfetched. And it'll sit on the shelf with the rest of the books about bad ladies that no one is interested in reading.'

Q.

'The world only likes certain types of monsters, and women ain't it. They're society's back bone, or touch stone if you like; they're the reminder that mankind and womankind are two separate breeds entirely and that's why people can't handle it, when women balls up, I mean. We need to believe in a higher power that lords it over men and although they won't have it, men, that is, the higher power, moral high-ground, pedestal-perchers, well, that's women. And that's why when they do go tits up with something, and the world bravely decides to acknowledge it for once, that's why we all have such a hard time coming to terms with it. But, but why, a woman can't possibly do such a thing, everyone cries. Because that's what we tell ourselves, isn't it, that's what we need to believe.'

Q.

'No, love, not just as bad as men. Worse than. We're naturally malicious, cunning, secretive, even our genitals stay tucked out of the way and if that doesn't seem suspect then I don't know what does. Women don't like serving things up front anymore. Maybe they did, but we're going back some years now, probably to the days when men were still gentlemen rather than lads; that's when women were women, rather than bitches. You're shaking your head; you don't agree?'

Q.

'If I can't say it about women then who can? Men aren't allowed to say shit these days without getting called out on it by one feminazi or another, and women are getting away with murder for it—not literally, no, before you say anything about that. But you know what I mean. One wrong word from a bloke and it's misogyny, woman-hater, blah blah, bollocks. But women? Men are all scum, let them come and make them leave, we don't need 'em anymore. And what are women who say that? Liberated! Empowered! Fucking idiots.'

'And don't look at me like that because you know that it's true. You're a woman, writing a book about terrible women, so you're in no position to defend them. Christ, you're trying to make a living off the terrible shit that women do. And that's fine, by the way, because there is a lot of terrible shit. I just like to think we're getting to a point, though, where we're allowed to talk about it openly, and that's what I'm doing here. That's why you picked me. Honest to a fault when it comes to my opinions; a little less so when it comes to cold hard facts, admittedly, but you'll mostly get the truth from me, love.'

Q.

'I could tell you some stories about the women in here. It's a stereotype these days that women gas a lot, and share a bit more than they really should. But, not so much a stereotype as a factual look at the female and her ways, I think. Let me tell you, and this place will vouch for it, if you put a group of women in close proximity with fuck all to do for a prolonged period of time, it will take, on average, a month for them to learn each other's life stories. They talk, and talk, and trade, and talk. There are some women in here whose names I don't even know, but I can tell you how old they were when they lost their virginities, and when it first occurred to them that they could kill their husbands. Stories galore, I tell you, but no, not so good with the names. Not that I suppose that matters much; you'll be changing them, won't you? Anonymity and all that. These women talk the talk in here but I'm not sure they'd want the great reading public to know too much about their unmentionables. There's not a whole lot to be proud of in these stories.'

'This is the first time that I've done anything like this, honestly.'

Brief Interviews With Hideous Women

Interview One

'I mean, what choice did I have? He'd put in so much graft that it seemed a shame to say no after all that, and besides, I would have looked like a right bitch, wouldn't I? That's the problem with this society, you have to be so careful of everything that you do and say to people because before you know it people are crying prejudice this and bloody discrimination that. Like I said, he'd put in so much graft and I'd obviously done something to make him think that he could trust me and I mean, it's just sex, you know, so it didn't seem like that big a deal.'

Q.

'Oh no, I don't have pity sex with people.'

Q.

'Well, you know, just ordinary sex. This is exactly what I mean, all these labels and bullshit that people need to slap on everything nowadays. You're making me sound like a bad person for shagging him, but if I'd said, sorry love, but you've got a gammy arm and I don't want you, your arm or your dick anywhere near me, I'd have been a bad person then, wouldn't I? Double goddam standards, that's what it boils down to. Men can still do whatever they like but I'm stuck between a rock and a wotsit, aren't I? You'd think after all those women burning their bras and whatever else they did, you know, you'd think that things had changed and things would be better but no, I'm still a slag for sleeping with someone that I don't particularly fancy, whether I did it for pity or sympathy or whatever else, and shit, no wonder those feminists are so angry.'

Q.

'Of course. I'm a woman, aren't I? I don't think you can be a woman in this day and age and not be a feminist or whatever.'

Q.

'My idea of equality? Well, we're better than men, aren't we? And it's about time they bloody realised. Like, this bloke that I went out with, he wasn't even that good but somehow he managed to have me and two others on the go at once and no one bats a bloody eyelid. But I do it, well, I did it, and I know that I'm good at it, like I know it, loads of people have told me, but suddenly like, I'm out of order and I'm the one that needs to learn her place and respect her man and all this other shit, like he ever respects me. So that's my idea of equality, women being able to sleep with whoever they want and men learning some respect; they should realise they're lucky to have one woman. Yeah, that's it.'

Q.

'The Suffragettes? I haven't had any run-ins with 'em, are you sure they're on this estate?'

Interview Two

'It wasn't really open for debate. Given that I didn't want to have children in the first place, it seemed fair that when I'd squeezed three out, I went back to work and hubby starting changing nappies. It's hardly a glamorous life for him, I know, but he seemed to think that it was good enough for me. Frankly, I would have had my tubes tied long ago if my doctor would have just signed the paperwork for it, rather than feeding me this drivel about how I might change my mind in the future. I didn't realise that when he said I might change my mind, what he actually meant was my husband would change my mind for me. But I suppose that's male solidarity for you, isn't it?'

Q.

'Christ no, I love being a working mother. What exactly am I missing out on? Snotty noses, bad school reports, and the chance to develop a dysfunctional relationship with my three children, because their mother moved into their pockets for the first eighteen years of their lives. It's not healthy at all to have a parent there all the time, whether the child is five or twenty-five. Parents need some grown up time and children need some child time. It's the only way to maintain a working relationship between everyone in the family.'

Q.

'My husband? He spends most of his time playing with Lego and when he isn't doing that he's usually sitting in the sunshine at the park, allegedly keeping a close eye on our children—who manage to come home looking like they've been mud wrestling anyway—so what exactly does he need a break from? The kids have a harder life than he does.'

Interview Three

'I don't know what the problem is either, to be honest. You're everything that a woman could ever possibly want, and if my ex had behaved how you do then we'd still be together and I know we would, but when you're like it, it just annoys the life out of me. I can't explain it. Like, you tell me you miss me and everything, and you say it all the time, but I don't know how I'm meant to say it back when I don't miss you. Am I meant to lie about it?'
Q.

'No, never. When do I get a chance to miss you?'
Q.

'In your mind it's so simple! And that's exactly why I don't think things will work out with us, short term, long term, whatever term. Your life is black and white; you either like someone or you don't; you want to be with someone or you don't. My world is colour, like this massive mess of colour, and when I meet people whose lives are black and white, it's like you waltz in and just smudge me up until my colours are just this grey matter than I can't even decipher, and then you start asking me questions as if I'm meant to have the code that cracks whatever is in front of me. I'm not a code-cracker, I'm a riddle; I've always been a riddle and if you want to be with me then you're just going to have to crack me, or something.'
Q.

'I hate it when you say that. You boil everything

down to one seemingly simple question like that will fix everything, and if I can just answer that one question then everything will be alright between us. It's hilarious, really, because this is exactly what I'm trying to explain to you: I'm not a one question kind of girl! Have you listened to anything that I've said?'

Q.

'Because I've been here before. You want someone who can be domesticated, right? A little lady who will sit at home, maybe write the occasional poem, and then you can pat her on the head and tell her how well she's done, and how good with words she is, and how she could work with words for a living, if only she was married to someone who would let her have a job, and then you'd laugh at your own stupid joke. I can see it all now, and I've been able to see it for the three months that we've been together because you don't want a girlfriend, you want a wife and someone who can make babies. News flash, buddy, I hope you kept the receipt because I can offer you a life-time guarantee that you will find none of the above enclosed in this packaging.'

Q.

'See, and that's the other thing I hate. How should I know where we go from here? I think I've made it clear that I don't want to be with you, and I definitely can't give you what you want, so why do I have to be the one to leave? Because I know how it'll go. People will ask what happened and then sooner or later it'll come out that I was the person that pulled the plug and I know how these things get spun—the person who pulls the plug is always the one at fault, and I'm not at fault here matey, let me tell you that for certain. Anyway, why aren't you leaving, eh? Save us both the hassle of having yet another amicable discussion about where we go from here.'

Interview Four

'No, I've only ever had the one, and I can't say that it's an experience I'd rush to put myself through again. I didn't find out that I had got caught out until I was about ten weeks gone, by which point it was too late to have the tablet treatment for it; although, believe me, I went through every private clinic in the local area to find someone who would chance it. That's how it works, you see, if they can catch it early enough then there's some medication you can take and by all accounts it's like having a miscarriage. When you get further down the beaten track, as it were, then things become more complicated and you have to have a proper removal to see that the whole thing is taken away. I suppose, while it wasn't a pleasant experience I'll admit, it's best to make sure the whole thing is gone. Don't want any further complications down the road, you know.'

Q.

'I opted for a local anaesthetic; generals have always made me feel a little groggy, and from the information that I'd been given prior to the procedure, it sounded like I was going to suffer enough without adding something else to the equation. So yes, I remember the operation; if operation is indeed the right term to use for what is essentially a glorified Hoover.'

Q.

'To be entirely honest, which is, I assume, what

you want me to be, the thought never even crossed my mind. It would have been a great inconvenience, and that's putting it mildly. I'm a middle–aged woman with a high-powered career; it's not exactly unusual for me to miss a period. When I missed two, though, it certainly raised some flags. I took a test after what turned out to be eight weeks, which meant that I was already too late for the non-invasive procedure; my doctor gleefully told me that she didn't perform them anyway. Not her sort of thing, she said, as if it's anyone's. There's no point in me being sentimental about the whole thing, or looking back with regret. In fact, it was probably one of the easiest decisions that I've ever made.'

Q.

'They did say that complications could lead to me being hospitalised for an evening but thankfully nothing like that happened. I was released late afternoon, after having it done in the morning. So yes, I went home, technically. I made my excuses and went to stay with my sister for a week or so. I needed to stay away from home until the entire thing was properly cleaned up. You see, my husband would never have allowed me to go through with it.'

An On-Going Interview with the Narrator

Q.
'I think a big part of it is that a lot of women have something to prove, whether they do or not, you see? Feminism and equality and all the other buzz words have sort of hijacked things to the point where you can't behave in one way or another without accidentally pushing an agenda, and with that happening in the background everything has just become tangled, impenetrable. And, I mean, take some of the girls in here. They're looking for empowerment and by sleeping about they think that they have it. I might have missed something, but that doesn't seem like empowerment to me. When I was the ages of these girls, mind, empowered definitely wasn't the word for a girl who'd seen more pricks than a second-hand dart board. So maybe they're doing something right, maybe the world's wife does have a little more freedom these days. I'm just not sure she's using it properly, that's all.'
Q.

'I'm not saying it's okay, what any of these women have done; much as I'd like to I think that's a stretch even for the likes of me. But you can understand it, can't you? The world is split on how women should be these days, then the world gets ticked off when women aren't behaving right. As if one woman can tick the box of introvert, extrovert, conservative, and

sexual, and Christ only knows what else we're meant to have about us. Yes, it's hard work, and yes, sometimes women get it wrong.'
Q.
 'Some women more so than others, yes.'

She couldn't get the bloodstains out of her blouse.

(Not) Guilty

Suzanne wore what she considered to be a jumpsuit, a washed out denim-blue contraption that was flattering under no circumstances. Staring across at the woman opposite her, she felt almost ashamed to be in her presence, even more so given that this other woman had obviously taken her time getting ready that morning. Whilst, in a cell about seventeen miles away, Suzanne had merely rolled from her bunk, rolled (handcuffed) into the van, and then rolled into her solicitor's office. Or rather, her soon to be solicitor, she hoped.

After a week and a half in a cell, it was a shocking sight to behold a room that had more than cracked concrete to make up the wall decorations. Dishevelled legal volumes stuck out from their respective shelves, while some lay slumped on the corner of the lawyer's desk as she scribbled away, seemingly ignorant of her potential client's arrival. Suzanne passed the minutes by examining the room further; she observed the absence of any personality. There were no family photographs, no children; she glanced over the woman's hands: no wedding ring. She wondered whether she had discovered the reason behind this solicitor's Rottweiler reputation.

'I have your file here, but I'd like to hear things from your perspective, if you will.' The voice appeared from behind an inch of paperwork that the woman was absent-mindedly flicking through.

'If, of course, you've finished casing the joint,' she punctuated the sentence with a strained smile.

'I've been accused of murder and—'

'I know what you've been accused of. That's not what I asked.'

'Alright, my husband died of a fatal stab wound or two and the police think I did it.'

'You were in the house when it happened?'

'I was upstairs. We'd had a fight, which wasn't unusual, and I went to bed. He stayed up, like he often did when I was getting an early night, and that's when the break-in must've happened.'

'Were there signs of a break-in?'

'The back door was open when I went downstairs, so yeah.'

'Open? Not damaged, though? Were you in the habit of leaving the back door open?'

'It was what we'd argued about, matter of fact. My husband's a smoker and he was forever leaving the door open when he went out for a smoke, and I told him it wasn't safe, especially not in our neighbourhood, and it looks like I was right.'

'Convenient,' the solicitor replied, noting something down on the spread of yellow paper in front of her. 'You said you argued a lot. Did things get physical?'

'Once.'

'And who initiated it that time?' The woman continued staring down at the collection of papers on her desk, as if flitting between the police reports and the notes she was compiling herself. Her concentration was interrupted by the announcement: 'I went at him with a kitchen knife.'

The solicitor's eyes focused on the woman opposite her now. She removed her glasses and rubbed her eyelids, exhibiting something between exasperation and disbelief. Remaining silent, she flicked through the collection of police reports in the files in front of her before replying:

'There's not a police report for that incident?'

'The police don't know about it.'

'In that case, neither do I.' She returned to the paper in front of her and proceeded to put a collection of lines through the last four sentences she'd written. 'The knife that was used to stab him—one of yours?'

'It was from the chopping block in our kitchen, yeah.'

'So your fingerprints were naturally on it because it's from your kitchen,' the solicitor replied, speaking mostly to herself. 'Marvellous,' she said as she noted something else down on the sheet of paper. 'Continue.'

'They reckon I couldn't have slept through the attack or something; that's all they keep saying to me.'

'How did you sleep through the attack?'

'I'm a heavy sleeper.'

'Heavy enough to sleep through your husband being stabbed?'

'Well it looks like it, doesn't it?'

The solicitor flashed a smile. The room remained quiet, somewhat tense, as she penned a paragraph of notes alongside the ones she had already made. This continued for several minutes before she ran her finger down the file next to her, as if her next question was there.

'Give me your version of the whole evening, including when you found the body.'

'We were downstairs watching television when he went outside for a smoke, and he left the door open, again, and that's when the argument started. I told him he didn't care about us being safe at night and he told me I was overreacting. Things got a bit more tense than that like, but I don't exactly remember everything that was said—I can tell you it wasn't anything different to what was usually said, though. It was the same sodding argument on repeat. Or at least it felt like it.' She paused, giving the solicitor time to note down scraps of her statement.

'Continue.'

'I told him I couldn't argue with him anymore and that I was going to bed. He shouted something after but truth be told, I wasn't listening by then—you'd do just as well to ask our neighbours what he said, they probably heard it. May I?'

The solicitor lifted her head to see Suzanne gesturing towards a jug of water on the table, with two real-glass glasses next to them—a welcome change from the prison's plastic cups. The woman gave a gesture of permission with one hand as she continued scribbling on to the paper with the other.

'It must have been about one or two in the morning when I woke up, and I thought it was strange that he wasn't there, in bed like. He didn't usually hold on to his tantrums for that long, but I didn't really think much of it. I went downstairs to make myself a cup of tea, which is normal for me, at that time in the morning. And when I got down there, I found him.'

'Did you fall into a fit of hysterics and wrap yourself around him?' The question was said in a dry and entirely serious manner; nevertheless, Suzanne couldn't help but laugh at the phrasing before she replied:

'Something like that.'

'Well then what exactly? You'd just found your husband, stabbed to death in your kitchen, in the middle of the night, with a door wide open and a killer potentially in your house. Tell me exactly what happened.'

'It was a shock. I was in shock. I don't remember exactly what happened when I found him; I crouched down, I think, to make sure he was dead—'

'To check whether he was alive; not to make sure he was dead.' Scribbling again on to her paper as she coached her replies. 'You told the police what you've told me? You were in shock, and you checked whether he was dead?' Suzanne nodded her confirmation. 'So that'll be how you ended up with blood on your clothes.' Again it was said more to herself, as she continued noting down one thought after the next, simultaneously flicking through the police report as she did so.

'So they have fingerprints on the murder weapon, taken from your own kitchen; blood on your clothes; and the fact that you were in the house. Anything else that I need to know?'

'I reckon you've got about as much information as the police have now,' Suzanne replied, with an awkward laugh at the end of her sentence.

'Okay, I'll take your case, Mrs Lodge.'

The solicitor punctuated her announcement by slamming her pad down on top of her new client's pile of notes, as if clearing her desk ready for the next prisoner. Taking a moment to clear through the clutter that surrounded each pile on her desk, she soon met eyes with her client again, prompting her to ask:

'I'm sorry, do you yourself have any questions for me?'

'Only the one: why haven't you asked if I did it?'
'Because, Mrs Lodge, that's entirely inconsequential to my proving that you didn't.'

'I'm not saying that you're bad at it, I'm just saying that he's better.'

Oh, Oh, What A Difference A Day Makes

The woman and the man had been in a strange sort of relationship for thirty-two months and eight days. The woman, despite saying she was not ready for the commitment of a relationship, had been persuaded to try and have one anyway. She experienced what psychologists refer to as commitment issues, but modern youngsters refer to this as an uncontrollable tendency to 'put it about' more than one should (in regards to the phrase 'put it about', see also 'sowing wild oats', 'sleeping about', and being 'a bit of a goer'). Because of these commitment issues, or tendency to 'put it about', there had been moments in the aforementioned relationship with the man where the woman had struggled to remain faithful. There were also moments where the woman had not remained faithful at all.

The man, who had co-dependency, commitment, trust, and self-esteem issues, had always been very understanding of these moments of infidelity and, when the woman confessed, which she always did, he quickly forgave her and vowed that it would never again be mentioned, although it invariably was. While the man made a conscious effort to not mention the bouts of infidelity on the part of his partner, whenever a new instance of infidelity arose it was always a challenge to stop himself from alluding to the previous one, which the woman traditionally referred to as 'the last time this will happen'. Without thinking beforehand, the man would also refer to 'the last time this will happen' in order to build his case against the woman (quite rightly so, I think). However, the woman soon voiced her opinion on how utterly unfair it was for him to repeatedly return to an issue that he had allegedly put to bed; although apparently not because if he had then he wouldn't keep mentioning, now would he? Ultimately, after the fifth incident, the man vowed that he really would not mention the whole thing ever again, and that from now on he would just accept the woman for the liar and the cheat that she clearly was.

'You think I'm a liar and cheat?'

'I didn't mean that. I'm sorry,' he lied.

They progressed further in their relationship, with each party vowing to mostly ignore the flaws of the other. Unless, of course, the woman deemed it appropriate to remind the man of exactly why she felt the need to cheat.

'It's not easy being with you when you're like this, Harry.'

'Like what, Claire? You're the one who's cheating.'

'Because you're stifling me, and you're so damn paranoid all the time and I can't—I just can't take it anymore. You need to trust me!'

'I'm sorry, I need to trust you?'

Alongside the aforementioned issues, the man also suffered greatly from unrealistic optimism, which could perhaps account for his wayward decision to pursue such a woman in the first place. This optimism was (I believe) a prominent reason behind his tendency to forgive her many indiscretions. He would have perhaps benefited from the care of a therapist, had he had the available funds to enlist one. However, he frequently spent his free finances on presents and treats for the woman in order to soothe her guilty conscience.

'Claire, I know you've been giving yourself a hard time. Why don't we go out somewhere, eh? See if we can't cheer you up a bit.'

It was perhaps this aforementioned unrealistic optimism and his embarrassing devotion to the woman that allowed him to believe that after fourteen weeks free of infidelities—a personal best—that they had perhaps managed to turn a corner.

Feeling confident that perhaps their relationship was on the cusp of a new beginning, the man initiated sexual intercourse. He infrequently initiated this due to his severe and debilitating self-esteem issues; issues that were spurred on by his cheating partner who often used these issues as the underlying reason behind her having strayed from their not-quite-a-marital bed, which, somewhat ironically, made the issues worse. Nevertheless, as these issues had momentarily subsided, both the man and the woman optimistically grasped the opportunity to enjoy intimate time together.

'Just the usual, then?' Claire asked.

Assuming the missionary position for the first

thirteen minutes of the encounter, the man felt relatively comfortable and in control of the experience. The woman, feeling relatively uncomfortable and displeasured by the experience, proceeded to initiate a change in position, which resulted in her straddling him. After the ordeal had been completed, the woman lay smoking in bed, which she knew the man hated, while the man rested his head on her chest and waited for some kind of emotional recognition that would complete their physical connection. While the man had never felt comfortable enough to address the issue directly, he had always craved some kind of emotional response from the woman following their sexual endeavours, and he had always felt uncomfortable and pained by their absence. The man had always suspected that this was not something required from her by the other men in their relationship. In addition, the man would always recall one particularly emotional incident when, following their coitus, he had suggested they have 'a cuddle', and even offered to deduct this from his weekly allowance of non-sexual contact granted by the woman. However, the woman denied him the luxury, which she considered to be a pointless post-sex activity.

'A cuddle?' she laughed. 'Why would we cuddle, Harry?'

'I don't know. People do they, don't they? To get closer?'

'We've just been as close as we can get to each

other. That's close enough.'

'I just thought,' he paused, hesitated. 'I thought it would be nice hold you.'

'Oh, Harry, stop being such a woman about it all, would you.'

A severe (and understandable, if you ask me) emotional breakdown had followed that particular incident.

Ten minutes passed before the woman fell asleep, unconsciously shoving the man away from her and onto his cold and empty edge of the bed.

The man could never sleep particularly well after coitus. While the woman slept, he often found himself lying awake and over-analysing every thrust and grunt for hours after the event. The underlying cause for this being, although the man would never comfortably admit this, his concern that perhaps she was not sexually satisfied enough to remain faithful; which would, of course, be entirely his fault. The man watched the woman sleep for three hours and thirty-eight minutes before falling asleep himself. He anticipated that the woman would, as she usually did following a sexual encounter, wake him early the following morning and request breakfast in bed, which he always provided as a sign of his gratitude. However, the man actually stirred from sleep of his own accord late the following morning to find the bed was empty. Where the woman's head would ordinarily be positioned, there was instead a short, blunt, and rather soul-destroying note in its place.

Infidelity had escalated to total abandonment.

She shovelled the pills into the old woman's mouth, privately wondering what would happen if she gave her too many.

Mercy, Mercy

'Mrs Thornbury—'

'No, sorry, I'm a Miss,' she interrupted. 'Not a Mrs.'

It wasn't the same as the court appearances she'd seen in fictional dramas, of course, but there were definitely some similarities. The jury looked at her, horrified, just like they would on the television, and that was one thing that seemed authentic, she thought. The prosecuting lawyer circled around her, marking his territory in a fashion, licking a stray speck of saliva from the corner of his mouth. Samantha Thornbury couldn't escape the feeling that she was somehow a piece of meat being sized up by a frustrated jungle cat. Not in an animal magnetism sort of way so much as a, I'm going to tear you limb from limb.

'No, Miss Thornbury? You mean to say, there is no man in your life?'

'Well there couldn't be, really, could there?'

The lawyer used his tongue to mop up another strand of spittle before continuing his prosecution.

'No? And why couldn't there be a man in your life, Miss Thornbury?' His nostrils flared to double their previous size as he put emphasis on her Miss/Mrs status.

'Well, I don't think my mother would have approved, and besides, I was always looking after her, wasn't I? I can't think of many, any, men off the top of my head that would be okay with a woman in her forties tending to her mother instead of tending to him. It just wouldn't have been right, or fair.'

'Do you feel you have a good grasp of what is right and fair, Miss Thornbury?'

Samantha Thornbury's eyes flashed to her own lawyer. They had talked about questions like these before; they were leading questions, designed to trick her into giving the wrong answer. Still, she said:

'Yes, I'd say that I do.'

'Interesting,' the lawyer paused, leaving her answer to hang mid-air for ten seconds or so before continuing. 'So, do you believe it would be fair to say that your mother ruled your life, to a certain extent, Miss Thornbury?'

'Well no, she didn't rule my life, but she needed to be looked after.'

'And it was always your responsibility to do that?'

'She was my mother and she was in failing health, so yes, of course it was my job to step up and take care of her.'

'Job? Interesting.' There was another pause while the lawyer referred to his notes that lay limp on the desk, mostly for decorative purposes. 'And did you have a real job?'

'Looking after my mother was practically a full-time job.'

'Yes, I'm not really asking so much in a practically sense, I'm asking in a literal one. So tell me, did you have a real job?'

'No, I didn't have a real job,' she replied, with the tone of a disgruntled teenager. 'I did, though, and what a worker I was. You know Monroes in town? The hotel chain? I was their head chambermaid, one of the best they've ever had, my boss always told me. I tried to keep working there for as long as I could but with her being ill, I just couldn't keep everything to the standard that I used to, and my mother taught me that if you can't do a job properly then you shouldn't bother doing it at all. My boss told me that he'd be sorry to see me go but he understood, and that—'

'So where did your money come from?'

'I'm sorry?'

'Your money, Miss Thornbury. The currency with which the average man, or woman, purchases necessities such as food and clothing. Where, if you can recall without too much inconvenience, did you get your money from?'

Samantha Thornbury took a significant pause, as if the effort of recollection really was too much of an inconvenience.

'Well mother got disability benefits and I was paid a token each month for looking after her. We managed, as a lot of people in this country do. If you're implying that I kept her on the breadline while she was ill, then you're wrong. The woman didn't want for anything while she was in my care.'

'Not at all, Miss Thornbury. In fact, the only thing I was trying to imply, as you so put it, was how challenging it must have been for a woman your age to be out of control of her finances. I imagine you earned much less as a carer? That can't have been easy for you.'

'Out of control of my finances? That seems like a stretch. I was in complete control; she wasn't competent to look after her own money. It was yet another job that got added to my list.'

'And again you refer to this as a job. Did you resent looking after your mother?'

'You're putting words in my mouth now—'

'Answer the question, if you please, Miss Thornbury.'

'Naturally there were times when I resented it, every carer does. At the end of the day she was my mother and I would have done anything for her, so a little resentment isn't exactly anything to write home about.'

'So you mean to tell me, that after giving up your profession and your social life, and any romantic life you may have had, you, a forty–' he searched through his papers. 'A forty-two year old woman, only resented the situation a little? You can be honest with us, Miss Thornbury, we're all friends here.'

'Your Honour, while I'm sure my learned friend has a point in these circular questions, it would be nice for the court to know what that point is,' Samantha Thornbury's lawyer interrupted.

'Quite. Mr Burton, make a point or move on.'

'Of course, Your Honour. Miss Thornbury, you

must be a patient woman.'

Samantha Thornbury dropped her eyes and watched her fingers tie themselves in knots. She knew that the man was trying to provoke her, to get a reaction out of her; she knew that he was doing exactly what her mother had done and she'd take it for a while, like she took it with mother, but eventually she'd crack because all people crack and then what would happen, eh? Look at what happened before.

'Miss Thornbury?'

'I'm sorry?' she looked up, confused.

'I said, you must be a patient woman.'

'Is that a question, sir, or are you trying to lead my client into a dialogue with you?' The defending lawyer interjected again. 'Your Honour, this is getting extremely uncomfortable for everyone involved and an utter waste of time.'

'Get to a point, Mr Burton.'

'I'm just wondering, Miss Thornbury, how a woman who was patient enough to look after her mother for such a prolonged period of time, managed to snap so abruptly. Can you explain that to me?'

'People just snap sometimes.'

'Yes, but people snapping doesn't always lead to cold-blooded murder—'

'Objection!'

'Withdrawn.'

'I can see what you're doing, you know,' Samantha Thornbury began to address the prosecuting lawyer.

'You're just trying to push me as far as you can so I snap with you how I snapped with mother; so you can show all these people what a monster I am. Well, I'm not a monster, so you just push all you like.'

'Did your mother push you, Miss Thornbury?'

'All old people push; it's their favourite pastime when they get to that age. They go back to being a teenager, I think; in fact, mother once joked about how the roles had reversed. Carer becomes cared for, natural order of things, something like that.' Samantha Thornbury stared down into her hands again, as if the right responses had been scribbled onto her sweating palms prior to entering the courtroom. 'If you've never cared for someone then you can't possibly understand how difficult it can be, you just can't.'

'So difficult that you would resort to desperate measures, you mean?'

'She was ready to die.'

'Oh, was she? You're qualified enough to have determined that, Miss Thornbury?'

'You didn't live with her, day in and day out while she was hacking her guts up over the living room carpet, pissing and pooing herself all the live long day. She was a vile woman to be around, not a patch on who she used to be. I did her a favour if you ask me—'

'Samantha, stop talking. Your Honour, I would ask the jury to disregard this line of questioning while I have some time alone with my client.'

'Your Honour, please, this is the first revelation this case has had and now my learned friend wishes the jury to dismiss it? We may as well throw the whole case out if he plans to object to every slip-up Miss Thornbury makes.'

'Slip-up?' Samantha Thornbury picked up on the phrase. 'I haven't made any bloody slip-ups.'

'Samantha, be quiet.'

Samantha Thornbury froze mid-response, her mouth caught in a perfect O, staring back at her defence lawyer who, for a split second, had channelled her mother; right down to the last thing she had said before Samantha Thornbury had smothered her.

'Oh, here we go, Samantha stop speaking, shut up Samantha, you don't know what you're doing Samantha. I thought you were a defence lawyer, not a censorship programme. I can say what I bloody like because I haven't done anything wrong. People kill people all the time, for worse reasons than the ones I had, and believe you me, I had plenty of reasons!'

'Miss Thornbury, if you don't settle down, I will have no choice but to have you removed from court, and we will be forced to continue this line of questioning when you are in a better state of mind,' the Judge said, in a surprisingly neutral tone.

'In a better state of mind? I don't think I've ever been in a better state of mind, Judge, but thanks for the consideration there. Take this down for your bloody transcript, why don't you: I. Killed. Her. I had a list of reasons as long as my arm and so I did it. She might have been a fragile old woman to look at, but upstairs she was as bitter and as sharp as she'd always been. Always bitching about the things that I hadn't done, never thanking me for the things that I had. She never saw the hairline fractures, never saw them gathering on the surface, never paid attention after she got sick, unless she was barking orders. Never noticed, never understood, nope, never understood how things fester; never understood how there's only so far you can push people, only so far before they crack and they do crack you know—enough pressure and people always crack!'

'Yes, Miss Thornbury,' the prosecuting lawyer repositioned himself in the chair behind his desk before continuing. 'So it would seem.'

A Miscarriage of Honesty

The first time it happened we were in deep trouble. I'm aware that that doesn't excuse it, exactly, but it half-explains it, I think. We'd been married for seven years—which I think is a fairly substantial stretch of time to be married to someone without any major problems arising—and then everyone started to ask about an itch. 'Have you felt it yet?' my female friends would ask, three glasses of wine and two months of marriage in. By then many of them were newly coupled—my husband and I had married too young—and they were seeking wisdom, I knew, but they were asking questions that I had never thought to ask myself, never mind found answers for. And so

I asked my husband:

'Have any of the boys asked you about an itch?'

Subconsciously he scratched at his crotch before answering.

'What kind of an itch?'

'I don't know, really. But the girls, they keep asking about the itch.'

'Oh, The Itch?' He enunciated the words as if experiencing a eureka moment. 'Yeah, the boys have asked about The Itch. They said it should arrive any month now, seven years in and all. Why, what have the girls had to say about it?'

'Never mind what the girls have said. What the bloody hell is it?'

And so he explained. The Seven Year Itch is actually a valid psychological argument-thing that suggests that happiness of a relationship will begin to decline after a couple have been together for seven years. It's also a Marilyn Monroe film, but George said he didn't think that really had anything to do with it.

'So what, we're meant to be miserable now?'

'Not miserable, I don't think. Slightly less happy, if you believe in that sort of thing.'

'That sort of thing—psychology, you mean?'

He laughed the whole business off and told me—in the reassuring tone that all husbands come installed with—that he'd never been happier than he was now. He was settled and comfortable and quite content with our life; amongst various other comments he made that, to me, translated to 'Our life is boring', which on reflection, is an interpretation that I still stand by. Nothing more was said on the matter, though. Our official seven year anniversary rolled around without so much as an off-the-cuff comment about what this could mean for our relationship and our happiness, and we continued as usual. Until the business trip three months later.

'Lou, I told you about it already.'

'You absolutely didn't. Why wouldn't I remember something like that?'

'Christ, I don't know. But I definitely bloody told you.'

We went back and forth like that for some time. Nothing was achieved, bar us both providing each other with overwhelming amounts of ammunition for future arguments.

'So are you still going?' I asked, post-coitus three hours later, when I thought the whole thing had been resolved.

'It's work, Lou, of course I'm still going.'

And he did. For a whole two weeks. I know what you're thinking and no, that wasn't the trouble. The big deep trouble came another three months after that;, out of the previous twelve weeks, he'd been away for business for four and a half of them, and that doesn't include the occasional overnight stays in the middle of the weeks he did spend at home. Nor does it include the dip in his sex drive. And the underwear that was wedged into the side pocket of his briefcase. Because when men go cliché, they go full cliché every time.

It was a late night, wine-fuelled phone call that I made in the end. I hadn't called with any plans or expectations for what I would say, or what he might say either. And as for what I did end up saying to him, I certainly hadn't planned that. He was so preoccupied with trying to get me off the phone, and I had these horrendous images of a woman being with him—like right then, as I trying to talk to him—that I think, perhaps, I half-believed he wouldn't even hear what I was saying anyway. And after that it just sort of fell out.

'I had a miscarriage, George.'

The phone line became so quiet that I had to check whether the call was still connected.

'A what?'

It was too late to take it back then.

'A miscarriage.' I said again.

George was home four hours later. He had questions, of course. When did I know I was pregnant? Why hadn't I told him? Did anyone know—had anyone even been with me? I didn't know I was pregnant, I told him, until I mentioned some 'women's trouble' to the nurse who was discussing—somewhat ironically—birth control options with me. I told her what I'd been experiencing and she brought in the GP, who sent me straight to the hospital, and that's where they confirmed it. No, no one was with me. It all happened so quickly that there just wasn't the time. Lie after lie fell out of my mouth with such an inappropriately impressive ease that I almost believed the story myself, which, objectively in terms of believability and credibility, was probably a good thing.

George held me until the sun came up that morning, breaking his grip only to move into the hallway and place a phone call to his office. He'd had to come home, he said, for an emergency, and he'd need a few days off as well. It was an issue that he'd rather not discuss, he said. After that we hid ourselves away for the best part of a week. George didn't go to work, he barely even took phone calls from them, and to avoid leaving me alone for a prolonged period of time we battled our way through our first online shopping spree together as well. Tesco brought all of the necessities to our front door and, just like that, I got my husband back.

As a couple we mourned collectively for the baby that never was—albeit in different senses—and we grew back together in a way that the made the whole affair seem worth the trouble. The miscarriage we kept between ourselves, until a friend of George's said:

'Bloody hell, you pair, talk about a second wind. What's your secret?'

And then suddenly everyone knew. It wasn't Martin's fault, of course. Like I said, we'd kept the news between the two of us, and even we had to admit that the rapid turnaround in the intensity of our feelings for each other was an unexpected side effect of what had happened. We loved each other more, I think, both having a sudden appreciation for what had been lost—again, albeit in slightly different senses. I can't excuse it, I know, but it worked wonders for my marriage.

The business trips stopped, and although we spent more time together, we didn't discuss the possibility of children becoming a part of that. Neither of us would say it, of course, it being too close to an admission of relief, but we had always been so careful to avoid even the possibility of pregnancy that neither of us were quite sure how a baby had been made the first time around. George had come close to asking, once, but had clearly thought better of it before the question had become fully formed in his larynx.

'Were you about to say something, love?'

'No, no. I was, but it trailed off somewhere,' he replied.

'Maybe it will come back. These things often do.'

'Maybe.'

But it didn't.

It's a difficult story to tell now because we were happy. You can see here, from what I'm telling you, that we were, for a time. Our lives reverted to how they had been for the first seven years of marriage and I felt undeniably smug that I—a simple housewife type—had found a way to beat The Itch, not that it was a method that I would recommend, of course. For the three years—yes, it really was that successful—that followed, we were perfectly content. George went out to work every morning and came home, on the dot, every evening, with a kiss on the forehead every night and a bouquet of flowers every Friday. This became our revised marriage manual, until one Friday—I have the date scribbled down here somewhere, I think—when he came home late, without flowers, beer hanging on his breath, and a dust of make-up on the lapel of his jacket. Business meeting, he said. Thought he'd told me about it, he said.

The following morning, while George lay in bed nursing a hangover, I crouched down in front of the toilet in our adjoining bathroom. I took the first and second fingers of my right hand and pressed them into my mouth, pushing and shoving at the back of my throat until my gag reflex took leave of its senses. I upchucked noisily—deliberately so, in fact—and wandered back into the bedroom, sweating and panting, to see my half-cut husband propped up on one elbow, squinting at me with only one open eye.

'Everything okay, Lou?'

'I'm sure it's just a sickness bug.'

We spent the weekend wrapped up together with me intermittently making myself vomit. On Monday George announced a business trip on his return home from work, and that was the first genuine hurl of them all. He told me to talk to the doctor, that it wasn't right that food was causing me such an issue. I told him that it was nothing, just a stomach bug that I couldn't shake; he said to see the doctor all the same, and call him home if it turned out that I was wrong. You see, the bastard sent me off without so much as a backwards glance while he ran into the arms of—well, whoever she was.

I didn't see the doctor that week, obviously. But I did see George's bank statements. And what a rude awakening that was. This was the first business trip, yes. But not the first meal for two, nor the first expensive shopping spree, and certainly not the first hotel visit. I checked the dates with my own and realised that while there hadn't been any overnight visits pencilled in anywhere on these evenings, there had clearly been an afternoon stopover with someone. After that I couldn't stop myself. I mean it; the whole thing became a compulsion. George didn't call to see how the doctor's appointment had gone, so I made a point of not calling him. When he returned home later in the week—far happier that I had seen him in months, which is something I heavily begrudged him—I had a meal for two prepared and waiting. And that's when I told him the happy news.

'That's why you've been sick so much?'

'Around eight weeks, the doctor thinks.'

'Christ.' He pushed and shoved the food around his plate. 'I thought—I mean, don't take this the wrong way, Lou, but I thought that we were being careful? After what happened last time, I mean, Christ, once is one thing but twice is—'

'Two things?' I tried to lighten the mood. I hadn't expected him to be happy about the news, of course, but I hadn't expected such brazen disappointment about it either. It felt very inappropriate to me that a soon-to-be-father who was married to the mother of his future child should feel like this. And I told him so.

'I'm not disappointed, Lou,' he said as he moved around the table towards me. 'I suppose I'm just scared. I mean, after what happened last night. And I can't believe we've got caught short, again, like this, I mean—' He looked down in time to catch me flinch at his phrasing. 'I don't mean caught short.'

'I think I know what you mean.'

'I don't think you do, Lou. Look.' He crouched down next to me and looked up into my eyes. 'I'm over the moon at the prospect of us having a baby. I'm just scared, after last time, of what this could do to us if it goes wrong. That's all. You understand that, right?'

In my mind things had been wonderful after the first time, so no, I didn't understand at all. But I told George that I did. I realised then how damaging the whole thing would be, could be, and so I worked around it as best as I could. We made love every evening, like clockwork, and we ditched all and any precautions—'Well, we hardly need them now, do we'—in the hope, in my hope, that a baby—a legitimate, real, will-arrive-in-nine-months baby—would be conceived. Instead, my period arrived.

Which was just another thing that I had to keep from my husband. It was okay, though, because he was still keeping things from me. Bigger and badder things, it turned out, than I could have even imagined. And they were unashamedly landing on our doorstep no less. Bright and early one Tuesday morning—George had been away the previous evening—Jackman, Carter, and Nicholls' well-crafted envelope landed just inside my front door. With a bill inside for a consultation regarding divorce proceedings.

I read the letter until I could recite it and with each reading I felt something shift inside my gut. That feeling, it turns out, was our baby dying.

George found me red-eyed and heartbroken on the sofa when he came home that day. He didn't need to ask what had happened, though, and I thought perhaps I had managed to successfully fashion the same expression that I had worn the last time I had delivered this performance. For an hour he quietly sat behind me on the sofa, his arms wrapped around me and his lips occasionally straying up to the top of my head to plant a small kiss there before turning away from me again, in order to rest the side of his head against the crown of mine. We didn't discuss what had happened. In a way, I never really lied about the second one; the whole thing was just implied. But George didn't see it that way.

You see, he called the doctor. Then a different doctor, and the hospital, and eventually a divorce solicitor. Unreasonable behaviour, they said, which is fair I suppose. I'm not sure that I should have been checking through his bank statements and business folders because yes, everyone is entitled to a private life of sorts. And no, okay, I probably shouldn't have pushed for the second miscarriage either. The first one, though, I will always stand by. You see, that miscarriage saved my marriage.

The pill popped out from the packaging and skipped down the drain; she put the packet back in the cupboard for him to find.

Brief Interviews With Hideous Women (2)

Interview Five

'I think that women, as the ones who carry the womb, and the ones that have to carry the child to term, absolutely have the right to have children whether their partner wants them or not. It's not a case of compromise; it's a case of women being able to grab back their rightful power as the child-bearers. It's a wonder that men even have any complaints at all about the process, given that it's a fine opportunity for them to have sex without a condom.'

Q.

'How can men not want children? It's in their DNA to pass on their DNA through any woman that will have sex with them; that's how it's been for years and that's how it is now, whether men realise it or not. All of them want an heir to their proverbial throne, some of them just need help realising it. My husband didn't know that he wanted to have children until I accidentally got pregnant. A few arguments later and now he loves being a father.'

Q.

'Well, I stopped taking the pill without telling him.'

Interview Six

'When I was younger, I thought it was bad form to keep a written record of the people that you'd slept with. It just seemed like poor taste. Now I can't pinpoint what it was, if I'm honest, but something about number thirteen was a game-changer. It probably sounds bad but he was so terrible, and I didn't know his name, so I jotted down his credentials—size, girth, any tattoos, on his body like, not on his, you know—because I thought this way, if I ever crossed paths with him again, then I'd know. It kind of became like a habit after that, I guess. Every time I slept with someone, good or bad, I'd draw a line under the one before and just write a little description of whatever I remembered, so if the opportunity came up again I'd know whether it was one worth taking. It's just like a sexual filing cabinet, trying to keep things in order.'

Q.

'If I had to put a number on it, then I'd say I'm on about one hundred and twenty, but that doesn't include everyone. I mean, there have been one or two that weren't even worth writing down and trust me, when they're that bad, you don't need something to jog your memory.'

Q.

'Yeah, the good ones definitely stick in your memory too, but it's sod's law that you never bump into them again. They're usually lads here on their stag do or something, looking for a final hump and dump, and I'm only too happy to oblige.'

Q.

'Well, there was this one lad, I only took him home because I felt kind of sorry for him; he was obviously the ugly one in the group, you know? There's always one, dragged along because it would be unfair to leave him out, which is kind of how I felt, really, like it would be unfair. So there we are, in my bedroom, I've got my back to him while I'm fumbling about for a condom, I turn round and the poor sod's only been and gone to the party without me. I didn't even touch him; I don't think he even touched himself! And then, to add insult to injury, he starts crying. Like, who fucking does that? Actually standing there, soft and sobbing in the middle of my bloody bedroom. To this day I still think I should have been the one in tears. So yeah, lads like that tend to stick in your memory.'

Interview Seven

'We met each other at the supermarket; hardly glamorous, I know, but these things happen in the strangest of places, don't they? I do honestly think that it was love at first sight. We both reached for the last French stick and we both stepped back at the same time, like, trying to be polite about it. It was straight out of a romcom. Then, probably ten minutes after, after he'd offered to have a tiger loaf instead that is, we bumped into each other again, reaching for the last pack of cheese spread. Honestly, you couldn't make it up if you tried. I backed down this time and said he was welcome to it and then, I still don't know why, I mean it was so out of character for me to do something like this, but I told him that if he came back to mine then maybe we could split it. I've never been so brazen in my entire life. I was shocked at myself yeah, but even more shocked when he said he'd like to.'

Q.

'I completely believe in fate, yes! And that's exactly what this was. We were meant to be there, buying French stick and cheese spread, at exactly the same time. I just know that we were. These things happen for a reason, and my horoscope for that week told me, specifically, that I should watch what I eat.'

Q.

'No, I've never really thought about his wife. I mean, I'm obviously giving him something that she isn't, so what is there for me to feel guilty about? Surely if anyone here needs to feel guilty then it's her; she shouldn't be such a shitty wife.'

She took out the black book and added another dash to the tally chart.

A Little Too Relaxed

Jeremy sat down on the bed. He rolled his shoulders in a vain attempt at loosening tense muscles before letting them slump two inches lower than their previous position. It was no use. After a day like today it would take more than a little shoulder roll to pull his mood around, but there was no alcohol in the house following the latest celebrity-craze-detox. He roughly rubbed at the back of his neck with his right hand for three seconds before dropping it back into his lap. A sigh fell out.

'What a fucking day,' he said, more to himself than anyone else. He hadn't realised that she had entered the room, was just behind him, in fact, assessing the best way to clamber on to the bed without disturbing him too much.

The mattress sank slightly behind him. She was petite—tiny, he often said—so she hardly made an indent on the surface itself; yet it was disturbed enough for him to know now that she was there. Without turning to see her, he could already picture her on her knees. He felt her soft body press against his back as she leaned in. Christ, he thought, not tonight of all nights. Whatever it was that he needed to pull his mood around, he was agitated enough already to know that an hour of making her feel good about herself just wouldn't cut it. And he knew her well enough to know that she wouldn't offer him much else.

'Babe—'

She placed a hand either side of his neck and applied pressure. The skin bent beneath her fingers as she began to knead at him, shoving muscle this way and then that as if beating the air out of it. A small moan fell out of his lips and his eyes widened in surprise; it had been an accident, an uncharacteristic move that he expected her to comment on, but she didn't. She must know it's been a hell of a day, he thought (giving her a little too much credit, if you ask me). As he moved to thank her she moved to kiss him; a small and gentle peck in the stretch of skin between his neck and shoulder, hidden away in a dip that she often referred to as 'The Nook'.

'This is a nice surprise.'

She said nothing in return, just craned a little further around him as if trying to assess his facial expression. His eyes were closed, his head tipped back, and following on from the speech his mouth hadn't even closed again; instead, his lips sat slightly parted allowing small puffs of air to escape whenever she hit a particularly tense patch of muscle. Whenever she found one of these—whenever she heard his puffs of air—she would move backwards and place an emphasis on her movements over that part. She would press down harder and deeper, and she would wait for a small moan from him to punctuate the movement, giving her permission to move on. When his shoulders had loosened slightly, she simply started again.

'You have no idea how much I needed this, babe. It's been a shit of a day.'

'Tell me all about it,' she replied.

And he did. Jeremy handed over the full details of his confrontation with his boss first thing that morning on account of a major client withdrawing a contract from the firm, which was something that had nothing to do with Jeremy directly, but apparently much to do with him indirectly. Someone on the team had let the ball drop with the advertising campaign and pitched something inappropriate, insensitive even, without Jeremy even casting an eye over it, never mind approving it, and just like that the client had pulled out completely. They said, and Jeremy quoted, that they 'wouldn't want to work with a firm that took such a flippant and offensive attitude to the female form'. Jeremy didn't even know that the advertisement was for, for Christ's sake. He continued to divulge details—the argument with his team that followed, the shitty emails that followed on from that, the incorrect sandwich filling when his lunch order turned up—all the while his partner sat behind him, intermittently rubbing at his shoulders and occasionally pressing her fingers into the concave at the front of his throat.

When I walked in he was already sitting on the bed. His shirt and trousers were somewhere on the floor, already waiting to be picked up and ironed, which would need to be done ahead of tomorrow's work day. Well, the shirt perhaps not but the trousers almost definitely.

It wasn't something that I appreciated often—I suppose I rarely had the opportunity to—but there was something beautiful about his back from this angle. The skin was smoothed, almost unmarked bar a tiny collection of birthmarks five inches across from his left armpit; it wasn't even a sizeable chunky thing, just a small collection of dots that made up something slightly more substantial. While I watched, I saw him rub at the back of his neck, sigh, fidget; the usual signs of a difficult day at the office. I wouldn't, couldn't ask what had happened. But I knew that he'd tell me anyway, given time.

I climbed on to the bed behind him. In the four and a half years that we'd been together, I'd never done anything like this before. He'd never expressed a desire or a want for it, although he'd done it to me hundreds of times. I copied what I could remember. One hand either side of the neck, working over the shoulders, down the back a little, back up again. There was nothing to it, really, and I wondered for a second why I didn't do this for him more often. Seconded by a more realistic thought: Why would I?

He spoke in whispers, punctuating himself with little catches of air that fell out by accident the harder I went at him, throwing much of my weight against his muscles. He's larger, you see, and I'm a little smaller—tiny, he often says, actually. He said that it was a nice surprise and just what he needed, and one or two other platitudes that we throw out when someone is trying to make us feel better, but not necessarily making a difference to our mood. The thought was there, though, and he knew that. When he finally said it—'It's been a shit of a day'—I asked what had happened. And he told me the whole boring affair.

One meeting or another, one bollocking or another, one wrong sandwich filling on the wrong bread which would undoubtedly trouble his diet-regime meaning that dinner out the following evening with work colleagues—of his, assuming that that was still happening after the day's events—would be a veritable nightmare when it came to him ordering something that would counteract the white bread—gasp, shock, horror—that he had had to eat today.

'White bread, Karen, Christ Almighty.'

I ummed and ahhed accordingly, concentrating more on the patterns that I was making across his shoulders than what he was actually telling me. I didn't need to know the answers; he just needed to think that, for an hour or so, he was important. He thinks that I don't know he needs that but everyone does, especially men like him. And so I appeared to listen, carefully and consciously, as he discussed his absolute appreciation for the female form, despite neither of us having a clue what the advertisement was for or what was so wrong with it, followed by a second lament about the travesty of eating white bread in the middle of the week.

'White fucking bread.'

I'd lost count of the amount of times he'd mentioned that bread by the end. I was trying, I really was. I was trying to listen and care and be attentive, and all of the other wonderful things that wonderful partners—wonderful women—are meant to do for their husbands. But while I was kneeling behind him with my hands around his neck, my fingers wandering round to the front of his throat despite my best efforts to limit them to his shoulders, there was one thought that I couldn't get rid of. One nagging little comment tucked away somewhere at the back of my mind and try as I might, I couldn't ignore it. I pressed the first and second fingertips of each hand into the dip just below his Adam's Apple and thought, just for a moment:

Sometimes, Jeremy, I really could strangle you.

The letter looked lonely on their dressing table.

Fancy Seeing You Here

Him: You're the last person that I expected to see here!

Her: Well, everyone needs to get food shopping, Martin. Although I didn't expect to see you in somewhere like Waitrose. Did you get lost on your way to Aldi?

Him: Anywhere that sells booze is good enough for me (haha). I suspect supermarkets make most of their money from jilted husbands these days. Jilted wives aren't quite the market that they used to be, are they.

Her: I didn't jilt you, Martin; I just did what I needed to do. I never wanted to get married and you bloody know it; if it wasn't for our Rebecca coming along I doubt we'd have got married at all.

Him: So I sucked you into it, did I? Funny, it's usually the other way round with that and all.

Her: I saw an opportunity to get out and I took it. It's nothing more than that.

Him: Oh, and where is this opportunity? He doesn't do the Sunday food shop with you, does he not? That must be a strike against him.

Her: Oh yes, because model husband that you were, you were always there for the food shopping, weren't you? Never missed a bloody Sunday wandering around Asda, not you, Mart. It was your favourite thing to do.

Him: So what, I didn't like food shopping. That'll

be why you left me, I suppose?

Her: Oh believe me, there was more than one reason.

Him: It's a wonder you managed to stay with me for so long really then, isn't it? I'm surprised you didn't up and leave years ago when our Becca was old enough to fend for herself.

Her: You're being bloody stupid now—

Him: Oh, I am, am I? And I suppose you new bloke—your opportunity—is never stupid, is he? No, he's too young to ever be stupid. Just about old enough to know everything, I'd wager, maybe that's what you like about him.

Her: You're making this sound like it was something personal; like I went off with him to spite you. You still don't understand, do you?

Him: I'm not sure what there is to understand. My wife hit forty and turned into a tart; I thought that was meant to be the husband's job, but you always were one step ahead of me (haha).

Her: A tart? That's what you think of me now?

Him: I think that's what everyone thinks of you now, love. Women shouldn't just go off and leave their husbands like this.

Her: Oh, but it would be okay if you'd left me, would it?

Him: Well, it'd be a bit better, yeah! People would think badly of me for a while, but not as long as they'll think badly of you (haha). Oh don't look so down-hearted, love, there's a strapping pair of arms waiting for you at home to make it all go away (haha).

Her: If you're finished, I've got food shopping that I need to do. (Moves to walk away)

Him: Matter of fact, I'm not finished.

Her: Too bad, Mart, because I am. If you've got any more slurs you want to hurl at me, then you know my email address.

Him: (following her) I said I'm not finished at all, actually! Where's lover boy?

Her: Mart—

Him: Where. Is. He?

Her: I wouldn't know; there is no lover boy.

Him: Oh! Oh, oh, oh! This is just too good. What happened, love? Did he decide mutton wasn't for him?

Her: I think you'll find I was the one who decided that, which is why I left you—

Him: There's my girl. Come on; come at me with your best shot. What happened to him? You chew him up and spit him out as well?

Her: Sometimes these things just don't work out, Martin. They don't work out and frankly, if I wanted to talk to someone about things not working out, it wouldn't be my ex-husband, so just leave it.

Him: Come on, I know it's personal but we've seen each other naked most days for the past twenty-one years, well, you know, apart from the last four months (haha), so I reckon we can be honest with each other about these things.

Her: He was just too young, okay?

Him: Too young? Nope, that doesn't fly with me at all.

Her: I don't need it to fly with you, Mart; I just need to you piss off.

Him: Piss off? Piss off? Is that any way to talk to your husband? C'mon, just tell me what happened.

Her: I swear to God—

Him: Now, don't get feisty, we are after all stood in the middle of a fairly upmarket place. I'll do you a bang up deal: you tell me what happened between you and Casanova, and I'll disappear. Well, you know, until the next time I bump into you in this fine establishment.

Her: It got very serious very quickly and it wasn't what I signed up for. Satisfied?

Him: Nope. Serious how?

Her: I really don't understand how this is any of your business, Martin. Why do you even want to know? Is your own life so dull since I left that you need to siphon excitement off mine?

Him: Oh, love, I'm having nothing but excitement. It's all snorting coke and casual sex since you left. I'm as happy as a pig in shit!

Her: You're a pig, all right.

Him: Why don't you just tell me, eh? Maybe I can make you feel better. I was always good at making you feel better, wasn't I? I had my special ways; husbands always have their special ways of getting round their wives—

Her: I'd rather not think about that, Martin.

Him: Oh? Well I better not starting talking about how you used to like it when I—

Her: For Christ's sake. His mother got ill, all right? His mother got ill and off he ran to tend to her every need; calling me every hour to let me know how this woman was, this woman who I'd never even met, and I didn't care. I tried to, I really did, but I didn't care, so I got out.

Him: Well... And here I thought I got the shitty end of the stick.

Her: Oh, save it. I don't need you to try and make me feel guilty, all right?

Him: I imagine you feel guilty enough, or you should do, at least. Christ, love, what a time to leave someone. Take it well, did he? (haha)

Her: I'm sure he'll be fine—

Him: Did you at least have the decency to call him? Or did you just leave him a copy of the note you left me, with husband edited out? Oh Christ, look at your face! You left him a note!

Her: He'll find it when he gets home. It didn't seem like a good conversation to have over the phone.

Him: (haha) That's thoughtful of you, love, really. So instead of having it over the phone, you decided to not have it at all? (haha) Seriously now, your behaviour is hideous lately, bird, absolutely hideous.

Scene close.

An On-Going Interview with the Narrator

'I don't know that you can put it down to biology. Some can, I suppose, there's always a case for it I mean. But I'm not sure that I believe people are born bad, myself. I think we're clean slates when we come out, aren't we, and then little nuts and bolts fall into place, or fall out completely in some cases, and then we are who we are from then on. I'm not sure people change much either, though, once those big decisions have been made. You might not be born bad but when you become bad I don't think you can steer away from that. Do you see what I mean?'

Q.

'An example? Look around, love. Half the girls in here are too young to be here but whether they're here of their own doing or someone else's, that's the big question, isn't it. Like I said, women have a hard time knowing how to act these days with one set of rules smashing against another the whole time. A lot of these girls, the young'uns, I mean, they're here because they got lost somewhere between being a girl and being a woman, and Christ, who can blame them for that? They see all this trite on television and in books—no offense—that tell them life rules or goals like they're gospel, then they go out and actually do it and the world has got bigger and better ideas by then on how to treat 'em.'

Q.

'There are the harmless ones, obviously. The ones who saw their mothers work through the men about town and followed suit, or the ones who thought they'd play blokes at their own game, only bend the rules a little better. You can hardly blame them for taking those matters into their own hands because, well, men have had it easier, only up until now, mind, women are certainly doing their level best to make up that ground. But I mean, some of them copy what they see and they make an alright go of it, but some of 'em, especially the really young ones in C Block, I'm never sure that they're in the right place if I'm honest. The world chewed them up and spat them out before they'd even found their feet in it and now, sixteen, seventeen, eighteen at a push years later, they're in here, and will be for a while, some of 'em. I don't know, to me the world has got a bit to answer for when it comes to women.'

Q.

'You're right there, yes, that does take some of their responsibility away. And it's only okay to remove responsibility from women when it serves a greater good, isn't it.'

Q.

'I mean, no one minds taking away female responsibility when the woman gets married—oh, pet, you don't need to do that now that you've got yourself a husband—or when she's ill in one fashion or another—oh, you know how these women can get with their nerves—because we kid ourselves into believing we're doing the right thing, then. Would a man ever get that treatment? Maybe, if women keep on the way they're going at the moment, but generally, as it stands, no. Men keep their social functions when they get married and they get told to pull themselves together when they're stressed. Not like us women. And no, I know, not all women, before you say anything. Some women keep hold of their responsibility all through their lives and their marriages and what have you, but I'd bet money that their husbands are quick to remind them of it when the cracks start to show.'

Q.

'There's one woman, lovely woman, just upstairs from where I sleep, and I don't know why she's in here because I've never asked and it's not my place to, but her husband was a cracking example of that, from what she tells me. He wanted her to be independent, until they had children, then she was stripped of everything bar looking after his precious little boy— the daughter they had, well, Christ, she never even mentions her more than in passing so I don't even know what happened there. But that's a fine, simple, straightforward example of it. Women are responsible, fully-functioning members of society. Until they're told they can't be anymore.'

Q.

'Because society broke woman. And now it doesn't know what it's meant to do with her.'

Hallelujah

When Louisa was seventeen years old, she made a confession to her Catholic father. During their time together on a Sunday afternoon when they would both devote an hour to reading the Bible, she opened a discussion to address the topic of her never having had a boyfriend. It had never been a concern to her religious family, who believed God would bless her with an appropriate partner at an appropriate time.

'When the time is right, the Lord will send you the One.'

However, Louisa took this opportunity to voice her concerns not about her disinterest in boys, but about her unhealthy interest in girls. Grasping the opportunity, while shock held her father, she confessed that while she should have been praying, she was instead spending hours at the end of each evening fantasising about a number of women. It had been happening for some time and it wasn't until she attended her most recent Church class, in which the topic of homosexuality was discussed, that she realised there was a name for her affliction.

Louisa had tried to resist the temptation for so long but she couldn't. So, plagued by the promise of Hell and damnation, she was turning to her father, the man who she trusted most in the world—after God, of course—to seek support and guidance about how she should proceed with these feelings and, indeed, whether pursuit of these desires in a physical form would lead to eternal damnation of some description. Was the Bible absolutely clear about that? Or was there some wiggle room?

For a happy ending, please see **Extract A**.
For a disgusting ending, please see **Extract B**.
For a more believable ending, please see **Extract C**.

Extract A: Louisa's father, Joseph—'A good strong Catholic name. That's why I picked him,' her mother had always said—eventually accepted his daughter's sexuality. As far as Joseph was concerned, religion was a medium of love and support, and any religion that refused to love and support a member of the flock based on their decision to love a person of the same sex was not a religion he felt comfortable being a part of. Louisa did consider explaining to her father that it was not a case of choosing to love someone of the same sex, but it seemed as though this may detract from his meaningful stand against religious judgements, so she remained quiet on the matter. The rest of his Catholic family soon followed this lead.

Louisa eventually became comfortable with her sexuality as well, with the ongoing help and support of not only her father but also her mother, Geraldine. While it was initially a shock to the community to see such a devout family remove themselves from the Church, there was eventually a reconciliation of sorts. Louisa gravitated back towards the Church, where she was accepted, thus prompting the return of her family. As time progressed the congregation not only became more accepting of Louisa, but also welcomed Susan, her new partner, into their community as well.

The couple had been together for three years and were welcomed and loved by their respective families. After living together for an additional year they decided to get married and, despite reservations, they did so in their local Church, with the company of their families and an obliging Clergyman who performed the ceremony.

They lived happily ever after.

Extract B: Louisa's father, Joseph, was disgusted. Their hour spent reading the Bible became four hours of him reciting it to her, repeating the extracts that addressed the practices of homosexuals and the inevitable burning Hell fire that would follow their actions.

'We won't have it. Not in this household,' Joseph said.

Lou's mother, Geraldine, eventually became suspicious and, concerned by what could have detained her husband and daughter for so long, she ventured into their reading room where she found Lou crying, and her father condemning her. Geraldine demanded an explanation. Joseph announced that their daughter believed herself to be touched by Satan, and that that was not acceptable, not in this house, no.

Joseph knew someone at the Church who knew someone at another Church who could deal with these problems.

'One way or another, we'll get that demon out,' he said.

Geraldine agreed that treatment was necessary and so, the following evening, Lou was removed from her family home and transferred to an unknown location. Her eyes remained covered for the journey; when the blindfold was eventually removed she found herself in a bedroom with a boy who looked her age. The two found an A4 sheet of paper on the bed, on which was printed a series of diagrams depicting a man and woman engaging in coitus.

WE'LL BE WAITING AND WATCHING. PRAISE JESUS. HALLEUJAH.

...was printed on the bottom of the sheet.

The boy asked her if she was gay. Louisa had never worn the label before, but she nevertheless admitted:

'I suppose so, yes.'

The boy, who told Lou to call him Harry, was also gay. He had recently told his father about his sexual orientation, who had responded by sending him here, on the understanding that they would use a woman to remove the gay. Lou realised then what they were expected to do.

They protested, refused, and resisted, hoping that someone would take pity on their situation and release them. They remained in the room for six hours, until Lou, trying a different tactic, announced that she needed the bathroom. A response came in the form of a note slipped beneath the bedroom door.

GO IN THE CORNER LIKE THE ANIMAL
YOU ARE. WE'LL BE WATCHING.

For another four hours they remained inside the room until Harry suggested that they engage in coitus, for no other reason than to regain their freedom, satisfy their families, and attempt to recollect the shreds of their dignity that seemed to have collected in the corner of the room, along with their spreading patch of co-mingled urine. Lou declined, turned to face away from Harry, and attempted to sleep. She woke up cold and shivering, no, shaking. Harry was on top of her. A chorus of PRAISE JESUS, HALLEUJAH accompanied the assault.

Extract C: Louisa's father, Joseph, did offer reassurance, but not the type that she had been expecting. He informed her that she, like all teenagers, was going through a stage of experimentation; it was evil tempting her, nothing more than that. He himself had been tempted once before meeting her mother and he himself had resisted, and so must she.

Six months later, Louisa again turned to her father to seek reassurance as, after resisting temptation for so long, she was disheartened to admit that it was still a constant presence in her life. Joseph told her that temptation would lie in wait around every corner; she must put the object of her affections to one side and occupy her mind with healthier thoughts.

'It's a part of life, kiddo. You need to rely on God, cast out the Devil, keep your mind focussed. It happens to the best of us, on occasion, believe me.'

Two months before Louisa's eighteenth birthday, she engaged in coitus with her best male friend, Andy, who told her that he would help her become normal. They engaged in sexual intercourse thirteen times before Andy told Louisa that he was in love with her; she responded by telling him that they couldn't be friends anymore.

A month after this aforementioned coitus, Louisa engaged in sexual intercourse with Benjamin—'You can call me Benny,' he said, but Louisa never did—who was the boy seated next to her in Biology. Louisa initiated the encounter by asking how the human reproductive system functioned. Benjamin/Benny explained but Louisa said she didn't understand and asked if he would show her, so he did. It was a terrible experience, though. Louisa always sat at the back desk in Biology then, where she could be alone.

The third sexual encounter was somewhat out of Louisa's control. She did not initiate it, nor did she particularly remember it. It coincided with her first encounter with an alcoholic beverage and because of that, the behaviour of The Person was mostly unknown to her. After the third man, there was Claire. Louisa doesn't like to discuss that, but it may have been one of the best experiences of her life. Then there was Edward, Freddy, and George, all encountered over three nights; over those three nights, Louisa also discovered she had a passionate love of alcoholic substances, vodka in particular. She also discovered that, despite what her father had taught her, the music that was played in nightclubs was not the sound of Satan. Louisa developed a particular liking for music of David Guetta, and adopted the song 'Bad'—'Baby, why does it feel so good, so good, do bee da,' she half-hummed along while applying make-up in the Ladies—as her 'lady jam'.

Between the ages of seventeen and eighteen and a half, Louisa, following the advice of a friend she had acquired at the Genitourinary Medicine (GUM) Clinic, began to identify her lovers by writing a short description of them in a small black notebook that she kept in her bedside table, next to her Bible. Her father was under the illusion that it was a private prayer journal.

'It's good to keep a track of these things, kiddo. Always best to write things down, I reckon so,' her rather loosely reassured her.

After a year of pleading with her family—and making various cases for how the experience would deepen her general knowledge of life and the world around her—Louisa was, at the age of nineteen, allowed to go to university. Joseph was concerned by the corruption that lay outside of their community, so during their Sunday afternoon of Bible study, he questioned her desires towards women, voicing his concerns that the freedom of attending university may be too liberating altogether. Louisa reassured her father convincingly.

After another three months of living within the confines of her religious community, she moved the two hundred miles away to attend university, where she eventually contracted Chlamydia. Operating under the illusion that the pill somehow protected her from sexual infections, Louisa neglected to undergo testing for them. The Chlamydia she contracted at university went undetected until some years later when her husband, who had been handpicked by her father, began complaining of some rather unpleasant symptoms following the consummation of their marriage. Various conversations, appointments, and swab samples later, it was confirmed that both Louisa and her husband now had Chlamydia. Louisa was quickly reassured that it was treatable. But her now-useless fallopian tubes were not.

*She slipped two twenty-pound notes out from the back of his wallet,
but decided to leave the credit cards.*

Starting Young

Dad left. There's no point making an issue out of it because it happened years ago. I was five. It was difficult to begin with, but that counsellor woman that I had to see said that it's like that for everyone who gets left by a parent. I appreciated the effort she put in but I was five. My biggest concern was who would buy my jelly and take me to dance class on Saturday morning. They were Dad's jobs. Things carried on as normal for a while, minus one parent, but I remember a lot of the people in my class only having one parent already. It was a social epidemic by that stage.

It wasn't until I was seven that things really changed. Mum brought home Uncle Tony, and by then I had swapped jelly for fairy cakes. Tony never brought me fairy cakes, though, and I think that was a key reason for us not bonding as daughter and fake Uncle. Then Tony left—to my knowledge it was nothing to do with me or my intermittent demands for sugar—and Mum replaced him with Uncle Brian. He actually did buy me fairy cakes, but I see now that they were to keep me busy. Mum replaced him with Uncle Tom, who I only met once, and then I met Uncle Ricky, who was friends with Uncle Tom. Ricky stayed for ages, though. It was like having a Dad again, at times. He brought jelly and fairy cakes home with him. His friends used to come round and see Mum, though, and she would disappear with them while Ricky would stay with me.

'Nice to have some quiet time, eh, Squirt?' he would say and I would nod, too enamoured by the cartoon on the television screen to offer anything more.

Mum was always a little worse for wear when Ricky's friends left, though. I remember him hitting her once, and I remember her crying. Mum said a lot of stuff that didn't make sense at the time. Ricky left when I was eleven. He told Mum he was taking me with him. Mum kicked up a shitstorm over that, though, which was something that she spent a lot of my childhood doing, admittedly. She told Ricky that I was worth more. I was better. I needed more. I didn't deserve it. I should have a better life.

She started drinking a lot after all of that. She said the whole thing was my fault, but she could never really explain it all further than that. She stopped drinking when she met Uncle Derrick, though. I used to call him Grandpa Derrick and Mum didn't like that at all. But Derrick looked after Mum. I think that made it easier for her to look after me. It was still hard for her sometimes, though.

I remember, Derrick had had to pick me up from school once. When Mum got home she found us on the sofa. Derrick had told me to stay in my school uniform, and he had his hand on my knee. A little higher than my knee. Mum went crazy. Grabbed me by my arm and threw me into my bedroom.

I walked myself home the next day and when I got

back Mum was packing up my room.

'I didn't do anything wrong, Mum,' I protested, jumping to the wrong conclusion.

Derrick was buying us a house. A nice one. In a nice area. He told me that he wanted us to be a real family, and then he asked me to call him Dad. I told him that I couldn't do that because he wasn't my Dad. At that age I was yet to understand that what someone wants to be versus what they are doesn't always matter, especially when they have money to throw at you. Besides, Derrick married Mum six months after we moved. I had to call him Dad then. Mum said Derrick liked it, and I quickly realised that when Derrick liked something it made Mum happy. And it usually meant that I got a new CD. Jelly and fairy cakes were long gone.

When I was twelve Derrick bought me a mobile phone. Mum didn't even have one of those. She shouted at me then for being his favourite. It must have been hard, I guess, being over-shadowed by your own daughter. Put out to pasture by your under-age child. Derrick shouted at her for shouting at me, though. He bought me a laptop the next day and Mum moved her things into the spare bedroom shortly after all of that. And that's probably when I started to understand what was happening. Mum told me I was getting too close to Derrick. Derrick told me he liked being close to me. I remember thinking that this was the 'wanting different things' that had made so many of my friends' parents get divorced.

For my thirteenth birthday Derrick took me clothes shopping. He liked to watch me get changed. I liked to get new clothes. The more he watched, the more I got, and I liked that. In total he spent three hundred and thirty-eight pounds on clothes for my birthday. The next day, though, one of Derrick's friends came over to the house. Derrick asked me to try on my new clothes for them both and when Derrick's friend left, he gave me an envelope. There was one hundred and fifty pounds inside.

Life carried on like this for a while. I saw Mum less and less, but I saw Derrick more and more. We went shopping every Saturday for clothes. Derrick joked once that we'd need a bigger house, so I could have one of those walk-in-wardrobe things. He asked how I'd feel about moving, and he asked whether I'd want Mum to come with us, which seemed weird. They had an argument that night too, where Mum told Derrick to back off. They volleyed back and forth for time until eventually Derrick told Mum to get out. She left that night, but she came back the next day. Derrick was calmer and said that she could stay, but Mum was still sleeping in the spare bedroom. Derrick spent more time with me than he did with Mum by that point.

Two weeks before my fourteenth birthday, Mum told me that we were leaving Derrick. She explained that he didn't love me how he should. Derrick liked me how Jake at school liked me, and Mum explained that was wrong. I laughed a little and told her to tell that to my full-to-the-brim wardrobe. Derrick came in halfway through this conversation. I thought he'd be angry but he wasn't. All he did was ask whether I wanted to stay. And I did. Derrick was giving me a better life than Mum had, would, could. I got clothes, and other new things, whenever I wanted. I was a master of the game now. I could get whatever I wanted. Derrick had told me that a pretty girl like me could have the world.

Mum moved out the day after that. Derrick told her that she could come back to visit me on my birthday, but she didn't. Instead Derrick hosted a party for me. All of my friends from school were invited but Derrick said I could only invite five boys. With twenty-three girls coming, you didn't exactly have to be a genius to work out the reasons for that ratio. But with thirty-eight presents resting at the bottom of my bed on my birthday morning, I realised I shouldn't question it. Derrick and I nearly had our first fight on my birthday, though. One of the boys kissed my cheek and said, 'Happy birthday'. Derrick made him leave. He asked whether I liked living with him, and whether I understood that we had a special relationship, that couldn't be interfered with and did I understand that. Fourteen must have marked the transition into being a grown up because for the first time, I really did understand.

I went through some changes after that birthday but I didn't really understand what was happening to my body. And I don't think Derrick did either. One

Saturday, instead of shopping, he got a woman to come and visit me. She was really pretty. I asked Derrick who she was and he said, 'One of my old girls.' She taught me everything that I needed to know about tampons. And that during the week I was using them, Derrick wouldn't want to see me get undressed. I didn't really understand how she knew that, but she turned out to be right. She told me other things that I needed to know, too: never mention boys; never have girl friends who are prettier, or younger; make sure Derrick's friends liked me. She said this last one was important.

The week after, when everything was normal again, we went shopping for cosmetics. Derrick took me to a booth in Boots where there was a lady waiting to do people's make-up, and it only took half an hour. Derrick was disgusted, though. I looked at least four years older, and he hated it. I asked the woman if she had a make-up wipe. When we left I was his fourteen year old again. I suggested we go clothes shopping, because I was too young for make-up. Derrick seemed pleased with this. I even suggested that he help me in the changing rooms, but he shrugged it off. Apparently a public appearance wasn't as stimulating as a private one.

The Sunday after that one of his friends came over. Derrick asked me to do my usual fashion show, which I did for his friends quite often by this point, so it felt okay. I told Derrick I didn't like his friends seeing me, though. I told him that I was meant to be just his. I threw around things like 'special girl' and 'little princess'; the princess thing might have taken it too far, but he obviously liked it. He took me out of school for a week after that, and we went on holiday. It was the first time I had left the country. We went to Paris, which was redundantly romantic, but I went with it.

Derrick invited his friends over less frequently after all that. Which meant he spent more time with me. Which meant I got more things. By then I understood what supply and demand was, and Derrick wasn't stupid enough to not realise what was happening. Surely. Once, while he was working, I emailed him a picture of me still wearing my school uniform. He came home furious.

'Do you even realise how much trouble that could have gotten me into? It was a stupid, stupid chance to have taken. What if someone had been there, when I opened that message?'

He went on like that for a while but he was, ahem, excited, the whole time. It sort of took the edge off being reprimanded.

We played cat and mouse like this for a while; things didn't really change until two weeks before my sixteenth birthday. Derrick asked if I was ready to move into his room, but quickly reassured me that it would only be for one night. I was old enough to know what he wanted. And I was experienced enough to know he would be disappointed when he found out that I wasn't a virgin. I told Derrick that I wasn't ready, and he said that he understood. But a week later, before my sixteenth birthday, he asked me again. He told me it was my decision. I told him that I still wasn't ready. It hadn't been long since he asked. It was a big step. Derrick understood, or at least, he thought he understood. He suggested new clothes. They might make me confident. Loosen up a bit. Feel more comfortable.

Derrick spent nearly one thousand pounds on me that afternoon. But I still didn't sleep in his bedroom that night. Mum might not have taught me much, but I'd learned one or two things from her mistakes.

The morning after my sixteenth birthday party, Derrick told me it was time for me to move out. Move on. Maybe find Mum. Maybe move in with Benedict.

'You remember Benedict, don't you? He loved watching you. I'm sure Benedict would take you in, darling.'

Derrick had been seeing a new lady, and her a daughter. They were moving in, he said. It was time for a change.

She flushed the torn condom down the toilet and went back to work.

Brief Interviews with Hideous Women (3)

Interview Eight

'Well, the first one I had was when I had just turned sixteen and, let's face it, everyone gets caught out in one way or another at that age, don't they? You're young, single, and stupid, so naturally contraception is literally the last thing you want to think about. I mean, hello, can you stop and put a condom on please, talk about a mood killer. I lost my virginity three weeks before I turned sixteen and I had the abortion about two weeks after I turned sixteen. Bad luck, though, right? Getting caught out on your first time, I mean. I bet that hardly ever happens.'

Q.

'Oh right, the second one. I was… twenty-one, I think? So it was quite a while after I'd had the first one. I'd almost completely forgotten about it to be honest, until they dragged my notes up from the first time around and I was like, oh shit, yeah, that did happen. People forget all the time though, you know? It's hardly something anyone would ever want to remember. When I went in for the second one I was further along than the first time, that meant that they couldn't just give me the tablets for it, they said they'd need to do a procedure or whatever. It was pretty grim, to be honest. They like, I don't know how to explain it without sounding gross but they like shove this thing in and literally suck everything out. It's like a weird spring clean or something.'

Q.

'No, I definitely preferred the way they did it the first time. I told my friend, one of my friends came with me so I wasn't on my own for it or whatever, I told her that if I had to go through it again then I'd definitely make sure that I went early enough to get the medication for it, rather than the sucky thing.'

Q.

'Well no, obviously I didn't plan to have another one, I mean, Christ, who plans to have an abortion, you know? At the time I was just talking hypothetically and saying if, for whatever reason, I had to have another, then I'd make sure I went earlier. I was just being prepared like.'

Q.

'I don't really count the third one as a proper abortion.'

Q.

'Well it was proper in the sense that I had an abortion, but I was away when it happened. I was doing this summer abroad thing with a load of girlfriends and there were just blokes galore, like, all the time. We were there for nearly four months and after two months I'd already missed a period, so I think I must have got it pretty soon after I arrived. Anyway, it was all over in a flash but that was definitely the worst one out of the bunch. Bloody foreigners like, it was absolutely barbaric; I'm pretty sure they just swished a coat hanger about up there or something. But whatever, that was a long time ago.'

Interview Nine

'I personally don't like the word nymphomaniac. I think, over recent years especially, it's attracted an awful lot of stigma from people who inaccurately use it and, despite me possibly identifying with many of the debilitating symptoms of that state, I would still be loathe to attach the name to myself. Even the inclusion of the 'maniac' element warrants further attention, as far as I'm concerned. From a feminist perspective, it's awfully frustrating that a young, healthy, and attractive woman such as myself can't enjoy an active sex-life without being branded as some kind of tart, and the only way to escape that social branding is to instead brand myself as some sort of maniac with a mental and physical health problem instead. Where, I ask you, is the fairness in that?'

Q.

'Well as I said, I'm a young, healthy, attractive, successful—I think I neglected to mention successful the first time round—woman who has the world in front of her. I see no need to brand myself as anything more than that, but I suppose that if I had to put some kind of tag to my sexual activities then I would say I'm extremely enthusiastic about the prospect of having sex with people I know, and sometimes people I don't know. I'm a busy woman, though, so there isn't always the time to make a new… buddy, shall we say? But there is, however, always time to go to a bar and find a man.'

Q.

'I'm checked every three months and I always use condoms, so no, that isn't a concern.'

Q.

'It's not at all a case of being attracted to every man I encounter, although the world would be a much better place if I was. No, you see from my perspective you don't actually need to be physically attracted to an individual to engage in coitus with them; all you need is a good imagination and poof, the rest just appears with time. If you want to have sex then any willing specimen of humanity will do. I would always choose taking home someone who I'm not attracted to and having company, over going home alone and engaging in… self-service, shall we say? Nothing compares to the real McCoy and if I can't find a respectable gene pool to supply me with the goods, well, needs must.'

Q.

'Actually, I tend to dodge relationships whenever possible. In the beginning, men treat me like I'm some sort of mythical being. The novelty soon wears off, though, and they soon realise that all the relationship is based around is sex which, I appreciate, must be difficult for them, but I provide everyone with a disclaimer on the first date, second date at the latest, so everyone knows what to expect. I just became so tired of having the 'where is this going?' and 'what are we about?' conversations, it became easier to leave romance behind and concentrate on what's important.'

Q.

'Women live in fear that their men are fickle enough to leave them for me which, granted, some of them probably are. Nevertheless, there are boundaries that even I won't cross and I'm afraid that married men, or even men in very committed relationships, are that boundary. It's difficult at times though, seeing an attractive man, ripe and ready for the taking but being entirely aware that he's somehow off-limits to you, which of course just makes him even more attractive. Even if in reality he looks like Quasimodo's cousin, once you put temptation in the way, poof, he's a Calvin Klein model. But I've learned my lesson and now I know that when a man is off-limits, he's off-limits.

Q.

'It's a silly story, really, but I sort of slept with my sister's husband. I suppose that was the straw that broke the camel's back in terms of me admitting there might be a problem here, although it wasn't so much a problem for me as a problem for my sister. It's difficult in ways that people just can't understand and while I understood why she was upset, she just refused to see things from my perspective in terms of how difficult day-to-day life can be for me when it comes to men. Take yourself for example, you're obviously a successful man, innovative, intelligent, and *extremely* attractive and… I'm sorry, did you say you were single?'

Interview Ten

'My God, what isn't complicated about them? I seem to spend my entire life darting between wanting to be with someone and wanting people to sod off and leave me alone and then typically just when I do find someone that I might be able to settle down and have a thing with, I get this jittery feeling that maybe I don't want to be in a relationship at all, and it isn't even the fear of someone else coming along because, well, I'm not pretty enough for that to happen, so I can only think that it's the thought of being tied down emotionally to one person that makes me break out in hives because like, I just don't know how to process that.'
Q.

'You see, and that's the problem. I meet this brilliant guy who doesn't even want a relationship so I absolutely dedicate myself to changing his mind and making myself seem so awesome that he simply must want a relationship with me and then when he says, oh hey, yeah actually, I think I might want a relationship, I go, whoops, sorry buddy, I'm actually way too scared to be committed to one person so that relationship that you're now looking for, well hey, you aren't going to find it here, sorry again pal, make sure the door doesn't hit you in the arse on the way out.'
Q.

'I'm not saying that I have a fear of relationships

or anything like that because I know that sounds really unhealthy and probably is really unhealthy, I'm just saying that they aren't always straightforward for me and that sometimes they're more complicated than I even want them to be but it's like I can't help myself. I know I'm yammering here because you're making me nervous, because I get nervous whenever I even think about the idea of committing myself to just one person, like one penis or whatever, for a prolonged period of time, well that is nerve-wracking and, and I don't understand why more people aren't alarmed or nervous about it but all of these people around me are like, committing themselves to each other for their entire lives and, I can't even commit to the same brand of sanitary towel from one month to the next so how am I meant to commit myself to one person?'

Interview Eleven

'I'd class myself as an entrepreneur. Why, what would you class me as?'

Q.

'I suppose I'm a bit of an opportunist, yes. Women just make it so easy! Honestly, all you need is half an hour in a Pilates class—the natural habitat of middle class housewives—and before you've broken a sweat you already know who your best bet is. The trick is, you see, is that you get close to the insecure wife—a very specific breed of housewife. By the end of your first coffee together she's practically throwing you at her husband. You should meet him; maybe you can help us; we'll pay you.'

Q.

'Oh, that pretty much is the process! I take the rejected wife for coffee; I get her to pour her marital problems out and nod knowingly, before bullshitting my way into the role of Marriage Counsellor, Couples Counsellor, something like that. Yeah, I'm such a good listener; I love helping people; my friends always come to me with problems—blah, blah, blah. The wives just beg me to talk to their husbands then! I'm introduced as someone she met at the gym, or someone who she thinks can help. I meet them once as a couple, just to make sure they're close enough to breaking point, and then I suggest individual sessions, so I can 'get to know them as their own people'— they love that line. It's usually around the third or

fourth session with the husband that we end up having sex, although sometimes it's the first; it all just depends, you know.
Q.
'That's probably the most difficult part, actually. I mean, I get sex, which is obviously nice; well, sometimes it's nice, not always—you know how it is. But yeah, after that it's a case of seeing the wife individually for a few sessions, and they usually come in at around £100 a sitting plus a free dinner—it's such hungry work—and the husbands just sort of disappear from my range of vision. They pop back up at the end of every month when they make a bank transfer, but that's about it. It's the perfect business, really: while I'm fleecing these blokes, their wives are sort of paying me to do it.'

An On-Going Interview with the Narrator

Q.

'A little more about marriage? Pff, what more is there to say.'

Q.

'I have been, once or twice, yes. Well, more than once or twice. But you know that already. My first husband, Jonny, he ruined me a bit if I'm honest with you. There was something perfect about that man and I spent five years waiting for the catch but it never came. He was just a loving, decent human being. He could have done much better, which he realised in the end, but I suppose it was too late then. Five years had rolled by and that's a decent chunk of time to walk away from. Poor sod he was, though, I think he felt quite short-changed by me.'

Q.

'There hardly seems to be much point in talking about the others now. In one way or another they've all gone. That's how marriage works these days, though, isn't it, a temporary and expensive solution to problems in the relationship that just makes it harder to leave when the time comes. And the time? Well, that always comes. I don't suppose it's always a quick fix, though, sometimes I think people just do it because they're meant to; same reason people have kids, I suppose, because they've run out of things to do, or talk about, or argue about. That's why Fred proposed, or at least that's what I thought at the time, which is why I said no to him when he first asked. I've never thought much to the idea of doing something just because the world says it's the right time for it, you know, and although Freddy promised me that wasn't the cause behind him asking, I never quite believed him, even after I said yes. No, he was definitely one of my poorer decisions when it came to husbands.'

Q.

'Oh, love, I think it's best if I leave that story until a little later.'

[Interview paused. Interviewee requested cigarette break. Interview resumed four minutes later.]

Q.

'Oh, make no mistake, this isn't anything to do with age anymore. The young might be upping the game but the old girls are certainly doing their share of damage as well. My grandmother, God rest her, even she joined in the frolics before her time came, much to my grandpa's dismay. Watching her go off the rails, it was like, I don't know, it was like payback for all the years of ironing, and cleaning, and raising my mum and uncles, and all those Friday nights spent ironing shirts before grandpa went out with his work mates. It's like her 70s hit and suddenly, everything changed. She'd got all this energy, like raw feminine energy that she had to pack into everything she did. She actually became one of those empowered idiots, I suppose.'

Q.

'I'm not sure what started it. She went into hospital for a while with—let me think—a urine infection? It doesn't sound like much but when they're at that age, those things can be real problems. And everything changed. It was like a time at the bar bell ringing on her life, I think, and even though she pulled round from it she was never quite the same, and that's when she left Grandpa for Greg.'

Q.

'His brother.'

'You know how men are; they only get worse as they get older.'

A Portrait Of Old Age (1)

'I think it must be about ten to seven.'

The watch, that looked near on the same age as its owner, was perched precariously around a wrist that was two inches too small to be wearing it. Eyes that were eighty-seven years old squinted at the watch face before looking up towards the woman in the bed opposite. As if a silent query had passed between them, Marjory confirmed:

'I thought as much, yes. It's ten to seven, dear.'

The woman opposite her was ignorant towards the revelation. Glancing about the ward again, and then back to the lady opposite, Marjory repeated her announcement in the hope of finding recognition from the woman who may, or may not, have requested the information in the first place.

'I said it's ten to seven.'

Staring, confused, at the woman in the bed opposite, Marjory soon shook her head and began to skim through the magazine that lay in front of her. Engrossed in the diverse stories that her local newspaper regarded as news, she punctuated her page turning with tuts of disapproval. Despite being unimpressed initially, Marjory soon became fascinated by the reporting of a young kitten in the local kennels that had somehow infiltrated the institution and made a heart-warming friendship with an old Bulldog being detained there. Bending her lips into a smile, Marjory was pleased to see such a moving lack of prejudice in the local area.

'Marjory, it's time to check your blood pressure now,' the nurse interrupted.

'Isn't it just lovely? You don't see much of it nowadays, do you?'

As the cuff curled around her arm, the nurse ignorantly smiled in response to her patient's query as she punched in the necessary commands for the machine to follow. Waiting for the cuff to swell to the desired size, the nurse felt obliged to ask:

'What are you reading about, Marjory?'

'Overcoming racial prejudices in the local area. I never thought I'd see the day.'

Peering over towards the open magazine, the nurse said, 'What's that got to do with dogs and cats, I wonder.'

'Well this kitten doesn't care that he's an old dog; she wants to be friends with him anyway. I think that's just lovely.' Marjory smiled, staring down at the pictures attached to the article. 'And they say you can't teach an old dog new tricks.' Leaving the awkward sentiment to hang mid-air, Marjory began chuckling to herself, her giggles increasing in volume as she became more and more amused by a humour that had apparently failed to infect anyone else within earshot. After realising the nurse was not taken with her quick-wit, Marjory repeated the pun, in case it had fallen on deaf ears:

'I said, you can't teach an old dog new tricks.' And she began laughing again.

'Marjory, what tablets have you been given today, my love?' The nurse leaned in sympathetically and rested a trained hand across her patient's forehead in an attempt to get an idea of the woman's temperature. 'Marjory?' she asked, pulling the woman's attention away from the picture of the kitten, which she was affectionately stroking with one fingertip.

'All of them.'

'You're just feeling lively today, are you then?' the nurse asked, smiling as she shuffled about the bed, fluffing up this and that in preparation for her patient's bed time. 'I'll sort your bed out now, Marjory, so whenever you're ready to get some sleep you can just give me a buzz and I'll help you get settled.' Adjusting the bed so the mattress lay flat, the action was punctuated by the sound of something rattling against the floor. Crouching, the nurse soon saw a cocktail of medication coming to a halt beneath the bed as a rainbow of colours settled from the crash. Reaching beneath the bed, she collected the colours one by one, cradling them in the palm of her hand as she wandered round to her patient, who was now stroking the image of the Bulldog.

'Marjory, what are these?'

With a displeased sigh, Marjory dragged her eyes away from the dribbling dog and looked at the nurse's hand. She studied the tablets with precision and concentration for thirty seconds, as if performing a quiet inventory to ensure every pill was indeed still there. Nodding her head with each count—one blue, two pink, one yellow—she then lifted her eyes up towards the nurse and smiled; a wide, toothless, gum-baring, childish smile, and then returned to her animals.

'Marjory, I asked what tablets you'd taken today and you said all of them.'

'No, no, my dear,' she said, pawing the image of the dog. 'You asked me what tablets I'd been given. I've been given all of them, see,' she said, nodding towards the outstretched hand. 'You can see I've been given all of them because you're holding all of them.'

'And why didn't you take them, Marjory?'

'Stop using my name like that. Marjory this, Marjory that, why haven't you taken your tablets, Marjory? I'm beginning to hate the sound of my own name.' She paused and began to mimic something like a chewing motion, throwing her gums around an imaginary scrap of food. 'What am I having for dinner tonight?'

'You've already had dinner,' the nurse explained, her patience beginning to fray around the edges. 'You had dinner at six, Marjory, like you always do.'

The nurse fed the collection of colours into a paper cup that was perched on the edge of the patient's table before shoving them gently towards her.

'Nonsense, it's only just gone seven.'

'Yes, I reckon you're about right with that Marjory.'

'And you're trying to tell me that I had my dinner an hour ago?'

'Mash, green beans, and chicken pie. An hour ago.'

'Well if I've had dinner already, then what am I waiting for?'

'What do you mean, Marj?' the nurse asked, half-interested, as she continued to shuffle about the bed.

'What I said. What am I waiting for?'

The question, despite being relatively simple and straightforward, was enough to stump the nurse. In the absence of a clear-cut answer, she instead said:

'I'll tell you what, if you take those tablets, then I'll see about some supper later.'

'I'll take those tablets later, if I can have some supper,' Marjory said, smiling, content with her bargaining skills. Although she became disheartened by the nurse's reply, an eye-roll and a deep sigh, before she turned away and left the miniature ward.

Glancing about the room, Marjory dropped her eyes back towards her watch, using her other hand to pull the sleeve of her nightdress clear from the face to reveal the time. Staring again at the lady opposite her, who was now staring at the lady next to her, Marjory leaned forward slightly and announced:

'It's seven and fifteen now, dear.'

A Portrait Of Old Age (2)

Something absolutely, positively, was not right with the way the table looked. Hushing her husband, Janice paused for a moment of reflection before lifting the small bag of bones, which doubled as her left hand, and shifting the top of the box of Roses chocolates three millimetres closer to the book that lay parallel to them. Assessing the situation, she remained quiet for a moment longer before she said:

'What were you yammering on about?'

'Doctor's appointment, love.' Her husband paused for a reaction; he quietly wished she might actually ask about his health. The eyes of his wife may have been looking in his direction, but he couldn't escape the feeling that they were somehow passing through him. 'Never mind, though.'

'No! Talk, talk on please. It's titillating.' She dryly replied, easing herself back against the support of her adjustable mattress, smearing over-exaggerated expressions of discomfort across her face as she did so. Reclining, she closed her eyes and waved her hand in the general direction of her husband, as if to usher the words out of his mouth.

'I'll let you sleep, love.'

'Did I say I was going to sleep, Ed?'

'No, you didn't, love. Ah, I only went to see the doctor about these headaches.'

'What headaches?'

'The headaches I've been having, for about a

month.'

Janice apparently didn't feel the need to acknowledge her husband's last remark.

Discouraged, he continued: 'Reckons I need a scan or something. Wrote me out these pills to tide me over.' He paused to fumble about inside his pocket. His hand emerged clutching a green slip of paper with something printed across it. 'No chance of pronouncing them, mind. You'll have to look for yourself.'

Handing the strip of green over to his wife, he lifted his eyes up towards her and was greeted by the sight of a drizzle of saliva escaping from the side of her mouth, running over what appeared to be the beginnings of a thin grey beard. With each breath that escaped through her parted lips, a snore soon followed. Janice's husband retracted his arm and placed the prescription on her perfectly lined possessions that were resting on top of the table.

'It's not much of a visit for me, is it?' he said, jokingly, to the patient who was staring across from her chair in the corner.

'It's ten to seven, dear.'

Janice's husband smiled, not quite understanding the woman's reply, or why she couldn't exactly focus her eyes on him. Perching his head on his balled up hand, he remained quiet for some thirteen minutes while his wife's snoring punctuated his thoughts. On the fourteenth minute, it seemed that Janice's snoring became too much for even her to handle and, with something between a snore and a cough hopping out from between her lips, Janice jumped awake. With her head firmly indented in the pillow, her eyes scanned about the room until they rested on her husband.

'So everything went alright at the doctors then?' she asked.

'Yep, grand. Absolutely grand,' he replied, resentful of his wife's disinterest.

Rolling her eyes, Janice shifted herself to gain a better view of him before spitting out her next announcement.

'You know, Ed, sometimes, you're a right bloody woman with the way you go looking for problems with yourself. As if you don't have enough to bother yourself with, having me in here. You should be worrying about me, not yourself all the bloody time. You're fit as a butcher's dog.' With the simile hanging in the air, Janice pondered over it for a second before forcing out a quick giggle. 'A bloody butcher's dog,' she continued, 'I've got no bloody idea where that came from.'

In a moment of what Janice deemed to be emotional weakness, her husband reached over the side of the bed and grabbed at her hand; her eyes widened as if a surge of electricity had run through her. Sporting the expression of a kicked puppy, her husband retracted his hand with urgency.

'Sorry, love. Shouldn't have startled you.'

Turning away from her husband, Janice slipped

her head back into the indent of her pillow before closing her eyes again. Her husband watched her face contort into an impressive array of expressions, experiencing a quiet amusement at the sight of her spit drying awkwardly at the side of her mouth. Janice's husband had a quiet chortle to himself as the saliva evolved into a crusty white component that slowly intertwined with Janice's whiskers.

'Ed, dear?' Janice stirred her husband from his thoughts.

'Love?'

'Before you go—'

'Oh, you want me to?'

'I think it'd be best. It's been a long day and I need my rest, you know that.'

'Course,' he bluntly replied, feeling his resentment for his wife swell.

'So as you're going, if you wouldn't mind—'

'Yes?'

'Whatever that scrap of bloody paper is, straighten it up or move it.'

A Portrait Of Old Age (3)

The sensation of something lodged in her throat had been plaguing Dora since the afternoon drug round, which had taken place ninety-three minutes ago. The nurses had been in and out of the ward since, flustering about the woman who kept telling people the wrong time and the woman who couldn't get to the toilet yet. At least the woman in the bed next to her was being entertained by her husband for the time being, allowing a certain amount of peace in Dora's own corner of the room. Extending her skeletal frame, she reached towards the corner of the desk where her Styrofoam cup of water was perched. With three frail fingers fumbling around the curve of the cup, Dora attempted to pull it into her hand, but to no avail.

From across the ward, Dora locked her eyes on the new and seemingly patient male nurse who had entered the room. He appeared to be flapping about the bed of the woman opposite when Dora eased out a deliberate and exaggerated cough. Gaining no attention from the nurse in question, Dora coughed again, this time louder, followed by an equally deliberate, 'My goodness,' and a tactical rubbing of her chest, to communicate discomfort.

'Oh, I'm so sorry! Do you need a drink?' The nurse asked, abandoning one patient and taking up residence at the bedside of the other. Perching against the edge of Dora's bed, the nurse picked up the cup of water before placing the edge of it against the patient's lips, with Dora's hands soon moving up to relieve the nurse's of their tipping duty.

'Alright, dear, don't over-do it; I can give myself a drink.'

'Oh, sorry, I—'

'You can go back to Marj now.' Dora dismissed the inexperienced nurse, her fragile hands still cradling the cup as she sipped at the water, which was now room temperature after two hours of being sat on her table.

'Actually, Boy Nurse,' Dora said to the man's back. 'Goodness, those words hardly seem to go together to me, I don't know about you.' Dora paused to chuckle over her remark before continuing with her initial point. 'This water isn't actually very nice; could you get me something a little colder?'

'I can. Is water okay, though?'

'I don't care, just make sure it's cold,' Dora instructed, taking one last sip from the cup before contorting her face into an obviously displeased expression. She loosened her grip around the container as the nurse attempted to ease it away from her, smiling in a patronising sort of way as the nurse backed away, almost with caution.

'I don't suppose there's any chance of a snack?' Dora shouted after the nurse, who apparently didn't hear the request. 'Bloody nurses, it makes you wonder what they're paid for,' she said, interrupting the conversation that the man next door was trying to have with his wife. Dora couldn't work out if the woman was sleeping, or just disinterested in her husband's prattle.

'I know what you mean, Annie,' the woman replied, eyes still closed.

Dora moulded her wrinkled face into a smile before nodding at the woman's husband and returning to her previous posture of being slumped back in her chair, her head lolling into the crevice specifically designed to keep her neck straight. That woman had been next to her for three days now; they had discussed their respective health problems of bad backs and urinary infections, but Dora still couldn't understand why the other woman was always calling her Annie.

With her head nuzzled against her chair, Dora scanned her eyes about the room before letting them rest on the window. It had been eleven minutes since she sent the nurse on the mission for cold water, and Dora rolled her eyes at the prospect of waiting much longer for it to be delivered to her. Momentarily toying with the idea of ringing the bell next to her bed and demanding a beverage, Dora was soon pacified by the sight of the male nurse wandering in, complete with a jug of water and a plastic cup.

'I half-expect you to be covered in dirt when you came back, young man,' Dora announced as the nurse set the items down on the table in front of her. 'You presumably had to trek to the nearest well to get this, yes? You were gone for about that long.'

Refusing to rise to the remark, the nurse poured a generous measurement of water into the glass, which he then nudged towards the edge of the table, within reaching distance of his patient. With a rehearsed smile, he once again backed away from the space, prompting Dora to snap:

'And what about that snack that I asked for?'

'I'm sorry?'

'A snack. You know, something people eat between meal times, something they have when they're hungry, usually gets them through the day. Mind you, I'm not sure you'd know hungry if it bit you on the backside. Look at you, small slip of a boy if ever I saw one; I'm not sure what use you're meant to be surrounded by old codgers all day. No back bone to you at all by the looks of things.' The young nurse looked down at his toned physique and suddenly felt entirely inadequate, and somewhat embarrassed, by his apparently less than satisfactory appearance. 'So a snack, any type will do, if you please.'

'I'm not sure that you're allowed—'

'Allowed? What is this, bloody fat camp? You're meant to be nursing me.'

'I'll go and talk to the Head Nurse on shift at the minute and see if she can—'

'Oh I see, so you don't have the authority to feed patients? A boy taking orders from a woman; good God, what is this world coming to? When my Jerry was alive I couldn't boss him about for love or money.' The young nurse opened his mouth to interrupt the bile emerging from his patient but Dora pressed on before he had any real chance of interjecting.

'Or perhaps we need to fund your university malarkey for another four years before you're qualified to make someone a round of toast. I understand now. Go on then, tell the Captain that I want feeding.'

Five minutes later, in place of the inexperienced nurse, Dora was greeted by the sight of a large and altogether more intimidating woman. Sporting a uniform that was seven shades of blue darker than the rest of the staff, the woman waded through the ward carrying with her a crustless piece of toast on a paper plate, which she dumped on top of Dora's table. Studying the well-built specimen in front of her, Dora was both amused and concerned by how the nurse—who was presumably the so-called Head Nurse—had been packed into her dress. With the buttons straining across her stomach, Dora quietly feared that she might lose an eye, or perhaps something more valuable, if the dress, or rather, the woman inside the dress, decided to blow. Torn between being concerned for her safety, and her undying desire to make life as difficult as possible for everyone around her, Dora said the only appropriate thing she could think of:

'I didn't ask for toast.'

A Portrait Of Old Age (4)

Buzz.

   Buzz.

      Buzz. Buzz. Buzz.

'Yes! Christina! What is it that you need?'

'There's no need to bloody shout.'

The old woman lay at an awkward angle on the hospital bed. Her nightgown had ridden up and was now revealing the swollen and slightly misshapen knees she endeavoured to keep hidden. Throwing a ball of saliva around her mouth, Christina glared at the nurse for a second before bluntly saying:

'I need you to pull my night dress now.'

The young nurse tugged at the fabric, pulling it loosely over her patient's knees. However, the back of the nightdress stayed put beneath the weight of the old woman.

'I can't pull it down any further, Christina, not unless you lift up.'

Christina rolled her eyes back judgementally before closing them shut entirely. Dismissing the nurse with a wave of her hand, her frail neck, unable to support such a head, appeared to almost crumble against the pillow as her head tumbled into the centre. The nurse remained still at the end of the bed whilst awaiting further instruction. When no other demand was given, the nurse began to slowly walk away, the bottoms of her shoes creating an uncomfortable suckering sound against the floor as she did.

'I'll need a wee soon,' Christina announced, eyes still closed.

Backtracking, the nurse repositioned herself at the foot of the bed and said, 'Okay, would you like me to help you to the toilet?'

'I didn't say now, I said soon.' Christina moistened her mouth with a dreg of saliva before continuing. 'I could use a bloody drink, though. Someone could die of thirst in this place.'

The nurse tipped two inches of water into a plastic cup that was resting on the bedside cabinet—entirely within the patient's reach. Christina popped one eye open to observe whether her command had been completed; she contorted her face into an expression of premature disappointment, spurred on by the assumption that the task had been completed incorrectly.

Sipping from the plastic container, Christina paused a moment before assessing:

'There's something not right with that water.'

'Okay, I'll get you some fresh water then.'

'I want painkillers.'

'You aren't due painkillers, Christina,' the nurse explained. 'I can check your notes and let you know when you are due some though, if that—'

'Oh no, perish the thought you put yourself out and do your job, dear.'

'Okay then,' the nurse remained calm and

collected. 'Well if you think of anything else you need, then you can just press your little buzzer, which I'm certain you know how to do, and one of us will come running.'

'Come running?' Christina eyed the nurse up and down before continuing. 'You don't look like you've run a day in your life.'

'Don't forget to ring your buzzer when you need the toilet,' the nurse said, finally making her escape.

Eyes closed and head resting against the NHS-issued pillow, Christina soon slipped into a shallow sleep; conscious of the world around her, but oblivious enough to let her mouth drop open and allow the odd snore to escape through it. Occasionally opening her eyes, Christina took intermittent glances around the stale-smelling ward. On the fourth glance she saw her eighty-two year old husband, now perched at the end of her bed alongside her forty-three year old daughter.

'Hello, mum, how are you feeling?' Christina's daughter asked with a generous measurement of forced enthusiasm as she crept closer towards her mother, grabbing affectionately at her frail hand.

'I wasn't expecting you both,' Christina dryly replied, directing the comment more towards her husband than her daughter. 'But I'm so glad to see you, my love. Tell me, how are the girls? Is Sophie getting on all right at school? I don't want this distracting her.'

'The girls are fine; Sophie is fine, and she's doing

fine at university, not school anymore, mum,' her daughter clarified, with a sympathetic smile.

The conversation continued between mother and daughter in a similar fashion for around twenty-four minutes, while Christina's husband remained perched on the end of his wife's bed. In the absence of a conversation that involved him, he instead opted to survey the ward with some intensity, studying the other patients as he went.

'Eighty-two and he still can't help but look at other women.'

The sentence snapped Christina's husband out of his trance. But when he moved to open his mouth, to jump to his own defence, as it seemed his own daughter had no plans to, his wife continued:

'I wasn't even talking to you, I was talking to my daughter, so keep shut.'

Christina's husband had been sat there for sixty-three minutes when his wife finally addressed him. 'I thought you'd have gone by now.'

'Visiting doesn't finish until 8, though. So I thought I'd stay, in case you fancied someone to talk to—'

'Well I've got Claire for that, haven't I?'

'Mum, don't be like that with him. He wanted to come and see you.'

'I'm not being like anything with him!' she snapped at Claire. Quickly reflecting on her tone, she apologised, and said, 'It's your bloody father, dear, not you.'

'I better be heading off,' Christina's husband quickly announced, desperate to excuse himself from the situation.

'I'll meet you at the car, dad, if that's alright with you?'

'Of course, mate, that's fine. You come down whenever you're ready,' he said, squeezing his daughter's shoulder in a fatherly manner. 'I'll come and see you tomorrow, love, with the kids, because they're planning on coming up to see us both. Unless you'd prefer we didn't?'

'It'll be nice to see the kids,' Christina replied, throwing no scrap of emotion to her husband. 'You don't have to come, though.'

'Mum, don't.'

'I'll see you tomorrow then, love,' her husband replied, leaning in to punctuate his sentence with a kiss on his wife's forehead. As he pulled away, he saw cold eyes looking up at him. Hurt by his wife's silent reply, he pulled away, nodded in the direction of his daughter, and began to shuffle out of the ward, tensing his tear ducts as he left to retain the tears until he was a safe distance away from his wife.

'See, not even a backwards bloody glance in my direction.' He heard his wife's voice travel down the corridor after him.

'It's not me, it's you.'

You Are Saying…

'It really isn't anything that you've done,' knowing that you're lying to the poor bloke who's sat whimpering in front of you. You repeatedly remind him what a wonderful guy he is, successfully glazing over the fact that if that were the truth, then you wouldn't be dumping him. And you also choose to tactfully ignore questions such as:

What can I do to change your mind?
How can I make this right?
How can I fix things?

Is this because my mother said she doesn't like you?

You resist providing answers such as:

Nothing, my mind is made up and it has been made up for a while, I just didn't have the balls to tell you.

You can't make things right or fix things, because things are fucked, and I know they're fucked, because I'm the one that fucked them. On purpose.

And no. In fact, I admire your mother and her honesty, and I envy it slightly because I wish I could be as honest with you as she is. I wish I could tell you that this has nothing to do with your mother and absolutely everything to do with you.

But instead you say:

'Sometimes things just don't work and it isn't a case of changing anyone's mind or fixing anything. It's just a case of enjoying what the relationship was and then letting each other go when it's run its course.'

You have to hold in a laugh, because it would be an awkward time to find anything amusing right now. But you do have to admit that there is something funny about using lines that ex-boyfriends have used on you. You're essentially recycling break-up speeches and while you find that kind of funny, you also find it eye-opening, because you now know what they were actually trying to tell you during those emotional and longer-than-necessary conversations where you repeatedly asked what you could do to fix things. Don't worry though; you're getting your payback now, aren't you? On a man who has never done anything wrong, apart from fall in love with you. And how dare he fucking do that?

You can see tears forming in his eyes now, because he knows that you're lying, and while the humanity inside you wants to offer some kind of consolation to the poor bloke, you just can't really be arsed. You know that it's difficult to hear someone you love tell you that they don't want to be with you anymore because, Jesus, you've heard it enough times yourself, but you think that people should deal with it with dignity, even though you never did.

He's turning away from you because he doesn't want you to know that you've made him cry; you carry on staring at him, even though looking away would be easier on both of you, because there's something fascinating about a grown man crying.

Something fascinating about a grown man, who weighs eighteen-and-a-half stone and is six foot, five inches tall, crying because you no longer love him. And then it dawns on you, while you're watching this emotional car crash take place in front of you, that you haven't actually had the balls to admit that you don't love him; you've only just found the balls to tell him that you don't want to be with him. And then you silently pray to any deity listening that whatever he asks next, it isn't anything along the lines of, 'Do you still love me?'

He finally says something like:

You could give me another chance.

You could just stay.

You could learn to love me again.

Say you didn't mean it, that it was cold feet, or something.

You decide to say:

'After this, I think it would be you who needs to give me another chance and after everything I've said, and how I've treated you, I'm just not sure that I deserve that.' You pause here for dramatic effect. 'I've got so many issues that I need to work on right now that, I just don't think I can be the woman that you want, or the woman that you deserve.' And then you kick yourself, because you just know that his response will be:

'But I can help you. I want to help you! Just please don't leave me, monkey, please?'

You take a sharp intake of breath and he thinks

that you're trying to hold back tears. What you're actually trying to do is stop yourself from telling him to stop being so pathetic, and that you hate it when he calls you monkey.

'You're a wonderful man, and whoever you settle down with is going to be an exceptionally lucky woman, but I'm afraid it won't be me, Colin. You're too good a guy for me to ask you to wait for me. You deserve more, and I know that in time you'll see it.'

What you actually mean is that he's too good a guy for you to ask him to wait for you to finish fumbling around with his best friend from football, which you've been doing for the past three months. And even if he was okay with that, his snoring is still a fucking nightmare.

It's been four months since you broke up. You always knew that you'd bump into each other again, but you hoped it would be at a time when he looked like shit and you looked like a supermodel. Instead, he looks like he's walked out of an advertisement campaign for Gucci menswear, and the woman he's holding hands with he could have met on a bloody photo shoot. You can't help but wonder where he even met a woman like that, because he certainly didn't know any women like that when you were with him. Or, if he did, then he did a fine job of keeping them from you. And why would he keep them from you? There would be no reason to keep anyone like that from you, because you aren't a jealous woman. Although, as you're huddled in the frozen food section of Tesco, trying to simultaneously keep an eye on your ex-boyfriend and who you assume is his new girlfriend whilst also trying to go unnoticed, you might be suffering something that resembles jealousy.

You drag your eyes away long enough to size up a microwave meal that's been dropped in the wrong section of the freezer. But you've let your defences down; you've lost sight of the enemy and, before you know it:

'Oh my God, Ellie, is that you?'

You've been spotted. Your ex-boyfriend and his new size-eight girlfriend who you're completely not jealous of are now there. In your space. While you're still clutching the microwave meal for one. You have no idea how you're meant to respond. Denial seems ridiculous, but you don't immediately rule it out as an option. You could easily put on a foreign accent and plead ignorance. But instead, you swallow an uncomfortable amount of pride and say:

'Wow, Colin, look at you! You look great.'

Because you need to be the bigger person, just this once, at least.

An On-Going Interview with the Narrator—A Conclusion

'You already know my story, no point bothering anyone with that now. It's nothing by comparison to some of the women in here, some of the women I've mentioned. They're the ones that people want to know about. The tarts and the virgins. That's what women sell best.'

Q.

'People will know where the stories are from whether I tell you mine or whether I don't. You're a nice girl but don't think I don't know how you're going to sell this to people. Inside a women's prison, the monsters behind the make-up, some shitty tagline to neatly summarise how brave you are and how horrendous we all are and how eye-opening this whole damn experience was for you. Which I'm sure it was, mind. It's one thing knowing there are bad women out there, it's another thing completely sitting down for tea with one three times a week for four months on the trot, eh? It's a wonder you're making it out alive, love, what with my history and all.'

Q.

'People know my story. They read about it. They still read about it. Every time a husband dies or a child goes missing, people remember my story fondly as the benchmark for how fucking disappointing women can be. They roll out that picture, that black and white, heavily edited, insert bags under the eyes picture, and they plaster it across their front pages and they scowl and they remind themselves how traumatising the whole thing was. So traumatising that they must—simply must—revisit it at every available opportunity, and my, don't they.'

Q.

'What side of the story do you think they want? The side where I'm dominated by a terrible and all-consuming male partner in crime who was miraculously never caught, but who continues to dominate my mind to such a degree that I can't turn him in? Or do they want the medically diagnosable version, where some prick with more letters after his name than he has in it can sit down and tell them, biological defect by environmental factor, what's wrong with me and why? This isn't an opportunity to share my side of the story, love, because it isn't one worth sharing. It isn't one that I would want to share.'

Q.

'What, just for your own morbid curiosity? You didn't seem the type for that.'

Q.

'All I have to say about it is that I did it, and I regret it. Saving grace that that is, at least something akin to a conscience lives in the old witch, not that anyone reading this would believe it of me. I know what I did was wrong but I'm paying for it and that sets things right, surely. Karma-wise. But Fred had it coming anyway. I know that doesn't sound much like regret but if I'm going on the record for things then the least I'm going to be is honest. Fred had it coming.'

Q.

'No, his son didn't.'

Q.

'You make it sound like a deliberate decision to just kill men. Are you looking for a feminist spin? Like I'm fighting against the deep seated patriarchy that occupies every nook and cranny in our society? If that makes you feel better, princess, then you push for that but you've spent enough time with me now to know that that just isn't how it is. We wanted equality and now we're getting it. Sometimes bad people are bad women. Nothing more to it, love. Nothing more to it than that.'